Mary Anne Breaks the Rules

Mary Anne Breaks the Rules
Ann M. Martin

AN
APPLE
PAPERBACK

SCHOLASTIC INC.
New York Toronto London Auckland Sydney

No part of this publication may be reproduced in whole or in part, or stored in a retrieval system, or transmitted in any form or by any means, electronic, mechanical, photocopying, recording, or otherwise, without written permission of the publisher. For information regarding permission, write to Scholastic Inc., 555 Broadway, New York, NY 10012.

ISBN 0-590-48223-8

12 11 10 9 8 7 6 5 4 3   5 6 7 8 9/9

Printed in the U.S.A.   40

First Scholastic printing, October 1994

The author gratefully acknowledges
Peter Lerangis
for his help in
preparing this manuscript.

Mary Anne Breaks the Rules

CHAPTER 1

I was shivering. A gargoyle on the balcony of the castle wall sneered at me. Snow floated downward in soft, cold clumps. My tears fell against the jewels of my gown as I held the dying beast in my arms. I bent to give him a kiss.

I woke up with a mouthful of cat fur.

"Rrrrrrrrr," purred my kitten, Tigger, as he shifted position on my chest.

"Morning, Tiggy," I mumbled.

The dream had faded. I was Mary Anne Spier again, not Belle. And I was in my normal old bedroom in my normal old house in normal old Stoneybrook, Connecticut.

Sigh. Tiggy had made me miss my happy ending.

I yawned, rubbed my eyes, and looked at my alarm clock. It was twenty minutes before wake-up time. I thought about going back to sleep. Maybe my dream was on pause, like a videotape, and I could pick up that happy ending (I *love* happy endings).

Instead, I gently pushed Tigger aside and sat up. Glancing out my window, I broke into a big smile. I could not wait to start the day.

No, it wasn't a holiday or my birthday or the first snow of the year. School was not canceled. The trees had not sprouted dollar bills. It was just an ordinary Monday morning in October.

Well, ordinary except for a few things: I was caught up with my homework, not one person was mad at me, my boyfriend and I were getting along great, my family was happy, and the Baby-sitters Club was not overwhelmed with work. (I will tell you more about the Baby-sitters Club — or BSC — later.)

Oh, and the weather was gorgeous. The leaves were just starting to turn colors, but it was still warm enough to wear a light jacket outside.

Everything was just . . . *right*.

Not that my life is usually so awful. It's not. Okay, I admit, I tend to be a worrywart. My friends tease me for being so sensitive. I'm practically famous for crying at movies. (My boyfriend, Logan Bruno, says he's going to bring a squeegee on our next date.)

But on that October morning, I wasn't worried about a thing. I got out of bed and prac-

2

tically skipped to my closet. I had picked out my clothes the night before: a brand-new pair of rust-colored corduroy slacks, a blue button-down shirt, and a floral-patterned white cotton sweater.

That's my look — Neat Preppy Casual — and I *love* it. Especially compared to my *old* look, which was more like Elementary School Blah. Up until seventh grade, my dad insisted I wear little-girl clothes and keep my hair in pigtails. That was back when he and I lived alone in a small house on Bradford Court. You see, when I was a baby, my mom died. My grandparents agreed to take me for awhile because Dad was so upset — and they didn't want to give me back when Dad said he was ready. They finally did, but Dad became convinced he had to be a *perfect* parent, to make up for Mom. To him, that meant being super-strict.

Now I'm in eighth grade; I have a cool, short haircut; I live in a rambling old farmhouse with Dad *and* a stepfamily I adore.

What happened? For one thing, Dad began realizing I was growing up. Then his life changed dramatically. How? Well, it's only the most romantic story of the century! A modern-day *Beauty and the Beast* (but don't you dare tell my dad I said that). I mean, there he was, lonely and single (and strict). Then one day a

3

girl named Dawn Schafer moved into town with her divorced mother. I became Dawn's friend, and we discovered that her mom was the former high-school sweetheart of guess who? Yes, Lonely and Single Richard Spier. So Dawn and I got them together . . . and it was love at first sight. (*Second* sight?) Anyway, they married, Dad and I moved in with the Schafers, I got a fabulous stepsister, and everybody lived happily ever after.

Well, that's not totally true. The story has an epilogue, which happens to be the one slightly negative thing about my life. Dawn is in California, living with her dad and brother for a few months. And boy, do I miss her.

But even that isn't so bad. We talk on the phone a lot, and she *is* coming back.

Dawn was born and raised in California. She is pretty and *very* warm-hearted. Her face is freckled, and she has light-blonde hair almost down to her waist. Our personalities are quite different. Dawn's a real individualist who doesn't mind making waves. She's a health-food addict, she believes in animal rights and environmental causes, and she doesn't mind a bit if people tease her about her beliefs.

Now that she's gone, I must admit I don't feel quite so guilty when I eat red meat and junk food. But even so, I can't wait till she gets back!

Anyway, the smell of eggs and spices wafted into my room as I was putting on my shoes. I was almost drooling as I went downstairs and into the kitchen.

Sharon was still in her robe, making coffee. Dad was hunched over the stove, wearing a long apron over his white shirt and pin-striped lawyer's pants.

We all exchanged good mornings. As I gave Dad a kiss on the cheek, I noticed his great-smelling omelet looked as if it had been made of Elmer's glue. "It's . . . white," I remarked.

Dad nodded solemnly. "The chickens who laid these eggs were raised in total darkness."

Huh?

When Sharon burst out laughing, I knew Dad was teasing. (I am *so* gullible.)

"It's an egg-white omelet," Sharon explained. "Your father's on a health kick. He's reducing his cholesterol."

"Want some?" Dad asked.

"Cholesterol?" I replied. "No, thanks."

"Touché!" Dad said with a smile.

Welcome to the Schafer/Spier Morning Comedy Hour.

We stayed in a goofy mood throughout breakfast. Dad kept telling us how he was going to run the marathon. Sharon found her long-lost sunglasses in an oatmeal cannister (she can be very absentminded). By the time

I left the house, we were all giggling.

I was still smiling when Mallory Pike and Stacey McGill met me at my driveway. (Mallory and Stacey are in the BSC. Stace, who's in eighth grade with me, is the club secretary; Mal's a junior member, because she's in sixth grade.)

"What's so funny?" Stacey asked.

I shrugged. "I'm just in a good mood."

"I hope it rubs off," Mal said. "My morning was horrible. The triplets were doing food checks with their scrambled eggs and I lost my appetite."

"Food checks?" I repeated.

"Yeah," Mal replied. "You know, when someone yells 'Food check' at the table, and then everyone's supposed to open his mouth and display what's inside?"

"Gag me," Stacey said.

"Gross," I added.

But typical, I must admit. Mal has *seven* younger brothers and sisters. Sometimes her house can be a little, well, zoolike.

We crossed to the other side of the street. Three third-grade boys were approaching the corner — Jake Kuhn, Buddy Barrett, and Mal's brother Nicky. Jake waved to us glumly, but Nicky and Buddy were deep in conversation about something.

"Food *what*?" Buddy asked.

"Ahem," Mal said, glaring at them.

Nicky gave Mal a sheepish look. "Morning," he said.

"Morning," Stacey and I replied.

The three kids hurried ahead of us, Nicky and Buddy jabbering away and Jake staring at the sidewalk.

"Poor guy," I said softly.

"Who, Nicky?" Mal asked.

"No, Jake," I replied. "He still hasn't gotten over his parents' divorce."

Stacey shook her head. "You never do, totally."

We walked along in silence for a while. I thought about divorce. It must be tough. Jake's dad had moved all the way to Texas. I could imagine how that felt. Dawn, my stepsister, missed her dad so much that she just *had* to move to California to be with him for awhile, even though her life here is great.

Stacey is a Divorced Kid, too. Her dad lives a short train ride away, in New York City, so you'd think it would be easier for her. Well, it's not. For a long time, she felt pressure to run to each parent for every little thing — to prove her loyalty, I guess. And they placed all these demands on her, as if she were a prize to be fought over. Stacey finally had to put her foot down. Luckily they've talked it over and worked things out.

Come to think of it, Buddy Barrett's parents are also divorced. Only Buddy is getting a new stepdad in December.

"You're lucky, Mary Anne," Stacey said to me as we walked past Brenner Field. "You're the opposite of a Divorced Kid."

"What do you mean?" I asked.

"Well, you spent your whole life living with *one* parent and ended up with *two*," Stacey replied.

Hmm. I had never thought of it that way.

At that moment, to tell you the truth, I was thinking about something completely different. My boyfriend, Logan, was jogging across the field toward us.

I waved to him, but he didn't wave back. Instead, he lowered his head and charged like a bull.

"Oh, lord," Stacey said. "He thinks he's at football practice."

"Aaaagh!" I tried to run out of his path, but Logan lifted me off the ground onto his shoulders. "Stop, I'm going to lose my omelet!"

That did the trick. Logan lowered me in a hurry.

"Logan, where do you get your energy?" Stacey asked.

"Rechargeable batteries," Logan replied. He began unbuttoning his shirt. "Want to see?"

"Uh, thanks but no thanks." Sophisticated,

cosmopolitan Staccy, who was born and raised in New York City, was actually *blushing*.

Logan has that effect on people. He is so cute and charming. (Okay, okay, I'm biased. But it's true.) He has dark blond hair, dreamy blue eyes, a great sense of humor, and the sweetest trace of a Southern accent (he grew up in Louisville, Kentucky). He *is* on the football team, but don't get the wrong impression. He's gentle and normal-sized and not at all jockish.

In fact, he's a terrific baby-sitter, and the only male in the Baby-sitters Club.

Logan put his arm around my shoulders, and the four of us continued toward school. At Fawcett Street we met Jessica Ramsey, Mal's best friend and the BSC's other junior member. She ran to us in her own unique way. Most people run heel to toe, but not Jessi. She runs toe first. That has something to do with the fact that she's a trained ballerina. It affects the way she carries herself on the street.

Logan, for some reason, seemed to find her run hilarious. He decided to do a couple of awkward-looking leaps toward her with an exaggerated sweep of the hand.

"Log*annn*," I said. "Stop!"

"No, he's *good!*" Jessica insisted. "Do that again, Logan."

Logan's face fell. "Well, I was just joking — " he stammered.

"Seriously, you ought to take lessons," Jessi said. "You have a natural form . . . and look at your turnout!"

"My *what?*" Now it was Logan's turn to be embarrassed. As we walked into school Jessi kept trying to convince him, while we all cracked up.

The rest of the day was just as carefree as the morning. I got back a math quiz with a perfect score (yea!), our English class spent the period reading a play aloud (I had only one line — double yea! — so I got to listen), and we had a sub in gym.

The only bad part of the day was when Alan Gray brought a battery-operated, realistic-looking rubber hand to lunch and let it writhe on the crushed ice between the salad bowls.

Kristy Thomas was the one who . . . *experienced* the hand first. She was reaching for a salad, talking to Claudia, when she felt the slimy thing wiggle in her palm. She screamed.

Alan, of course, was watching. And laughing hysterically. "Can I give you a *hand*, Kristy?" he asked.

Kristy cannot stand Alan. She took off and chased him across the cafeteria. Kids cleared away to watch. Two teachers had to pull her off him.

10

Fortunately Alan was the one who got in trouble. As usual.

After school Logan was waiting for me at my locker. He does that every day before football practice, just to chat with me. (You see what I mean? He is so sweet.)

I noticed a cut-out magazine article sticking out of his loose-leaf notebook. "What's that?" I asked, pointing to it.

"Uh, my notebook," he replied.

"I know *that*. But what's the article?"

"Oh. Nothing."

"Logan . . ."

"Just something someone gave me. I haven't looked at it."

"Let me see."

Rolling his eyes, Logan took it out. His eyes darted up and down the hallway as he gave it to me. "You can keep it, okay? Well, I have to go. 'Bye!"

With that, he jogged down the hall toward the gym.

The article was from some dance magazine. It was entitled "Teen's Dilemma: Big Ten or Big Tights?" and it showed two photos of a high school football player. In one, he was wearing a uniform; in the other, a tight-fitting ballet costume. On the top of the article, Jessi had written: "If he can do it, so can you! Want to come to class?"

I couldn't help laughing. When Jessi sets her mind on something, nothing stops her.

Poor Logan. His friends give him enough grief about being a Baby-sitters Club member. I can see why he didn't want to bring the article to football practice.

Boys are so weird sometimes.

I folded the article and tucked it into my backpack. My friends were waiting for me in front of the school. The day was almost over. A few minutes of gabbing, a nice walk home, a couple of hours of homework, and it would be time for our Baby-sitters Club meeting.

It would be a perfect end to a perfect day.

I smiled. Life didn't get much better than this.

CHAPTER 2

"Mm! — mm! — mm! — " grunted Kristy Thomas, pointing at the clock on Claudia Kishi's desk.

"*What?*" Shannon Kilbourne asked.

"That's easy for *you* to say," said Stacey.

"Sounds like?" Claudia urged, as if Kristy were playing charades.

The rest of us were laughing. We all knew what Kristy was trying to say.

Kristy is like an alarm clock. At precisely 5:30 (not one second before or after) on Monday, Wednesday, and Friday afternoons she calls to order a meeting of the Baby-sitters Club. Or at least she *tries* — even if her mouth is full of Gummi Worms and all she can say is "Mm!"

"Very funny," Kristy said, after she'd swallowed. "Claudia, you gave me these on purpose."

"*Moi?*" Claudia asked innocently. Then she

reached under her pillow and pulled out a small, plastic-wrapped box. "How about English toffee candies? You can suck on them and talk at the same time."

"Ew, I can't stand coffee," Mallory said.

"Coffee ice cream is good," Jessi volunteered.

"I said, *toffee!*" Claudia protested.

"Uh, guys?" Kristy said. "Can we get down to business?"

"Aye-aye, sir!" Claudia replied, stuffing the toffees back under her pillow.

You can tell a lot about someone by looking at her bedroom. Take Claudia. From the paintings on the walls, the beads and string lined up on her windowsill, and the plaster of paris bag on the floor, you'd think: *artistic*. From the clothes lying all over the place: *messy*. From the wild outfits hanging in her closet: *fun-loving*. From her school photo, which is framed on her desk: *beautiful, thin, Japanese-American, friendly*.

And you'd be right about all of them. But you still wouldn't know one of Claudia's most important qualities: *junk-food obsessed*.

Unless you completely took apart her room. Then you'd find Ring-Dings under her hat, popcorn behind the easel, Snickers bars wrapped in a blanket, and on and on. She is an expert at hiding all of it — in her room *and*

14

on her body (she looks like a model). Why? Because her parents are super-strict about nutrition. (They're also strict about the "right" books to read, so Claudia has to hide her Nancy Drew novels, too.)

Claudia is the BSC vice-president. We meet in her room because she's the only member who has her own private phone *and* phone number.

Without that phone, the Baby-sitters Club would not exist. How does our business work? Basically, we gather from 5:30 to 6:00 and wait for calls from Stoneybrook parents who need sitters. (Our steady clients all know when we meet.) With one call, a parent can reach seven reliable sitters (*eight*, including Logan, who's an associate member).

We try to distribute jobs evenly. Although some parents (and kids) do like to have one main sitter, most don't mind the variety. That's because we're all nice people (well, it's true), but also because we talk about our jobs with each other and share information. In fact, we write about each job in an official BSC notebook.

We have *many* regular clients. I know, because I keep an updated list of them, plus a record of the rate each client pays, *plus* a calendar of all our jobs (with reminders about upcoming conflicts for each sitter). All that information goes in one place, the BSC record book. My job, as you can guess, is club secretary.

Claudia is convinced I have the hardest job in the BSC. But you know what? I *love* organizing information. To me, it's like doing a big crossword puzzle.

"Any new business?" Kristy asked.

Funny how that question quiets us down. Suddenly we looked like a math class. Finally Stacey, our treasurer, held up a manila envelope and announced, "Dues day!"

"Oh no, it's *Mon*day," Jessi said with a groan.

"Do we *have* to?" Claudia moaned.

"Can't we skip a day?" Mal asked.

Grumbling about dues is kind of a BSC tradition. We don't really mean it. But I'm glad I'm not treasurer. I wouldn't be able to stand the teasing.

Stacey just smiles and shrugs. She's so good-natured. And not just about the grumbling. About the junk food, too. You see, Stacey's a diabetic and she's not allowed to eat sweets. Her body can't handle sugar properly. (She has to give herself injections of something called insulin every day. Can you imagine?)

As treasurer, Stacey's in charge of paying our expenses: Claud's phone bill, gas money for Kristy's chauffeur (actually, her brother), and supplies for the Kid-Kits we take on our jobs (boxes full of toys, games, books, and puzzles). Stace is a real math whiz, so the job is a cinch for her.

What's Stacey like? Smart, friendly, and gorgeous. She has long blonde hair and blue eyes, and she wears the most beautiful clothes. If you see something in a catalog or store window that takes your breath away, chances are Stacey already has it. She says she picked up her fashion sense in New York City. That's where she grew up. Was she a lucky kid! I think the Big Apple is *the* most exciting place in the world.

"Hmm," Stacey said with a smile, peering into the bulging envelope. "Almost enough to buy that suede jacket I saw at Bellair's," she teased.

"Don't you *dare!*" Claudia blurted out. "Not unless you take me with you."

"I could use some new tights," Jessi said.

"I need sackbut lessons," Shannon added.

"Sackbut?" Claudia howled. I thought she would fall off the bed.

Shannon shrugged. "Yeah. It's sort of like the trombone. I heard it in this early-music concert. It sounds cool."

Shannon Kilbourne is the only person in the world who would even think of something like sackbut lessons. She's multitalented and interested in *everything*. At first none of us knew her well, because she goes to a private school called Stoneybrook Day School. She also lives way across town, in Stoneybrook's wealthy neighborhood. Shannon used to be an associate, like Logan. Now she's temporarily replacing Dawn as our alternate officer, which means she covers for anyone who's absent. We've all grown close to her. She's friendly and open, with curly blonde hair and the most beautiful, clear, blue eyes.

How did Shannon end up in the Baby-sitters Club? Kristy recruited her. They're neighbors.

Sigh. Just saying that makes me sad. I *used* to be Kristy's neighbor. We lived next door to each other, right across the street from Claudia's house. We've been best friends since our idea of conversation was "Goo." We even look alike — both petite, with dark brown hair and brown eyes. That's where the similarities end, though. Kristy is take-charge and outspoken, and she loves sports. (My idea of aerobic exercise is a walk around the bookstore.) She's also the most casual dresser in the club. To her, "dressing up" equals "not wearing sweats and jeans."

Kristy, by the way, is the mastermind behind the Baby-sitters Club. The idea popped into her head one day when we were in seventh grade. Boy, were our lives different then.

We were still next-door neighbors. I was living with Dad, and Kristy lived with her mom and three brothers — Charlie (who's now seventeen), Sam (fifteen), and David Michael (seven). Kristy's dad had abandoned their family right after David Michael was born. What an awful thing to do, huh? It sure wasn't easy for Mrs. Thomas. Anyway, one night Kristy saw her mom frantically calling around for a sitter, and *bing!* Kristy thought, why not have an organized group of sitters, like an agency?

Kristy, Claudia, Stacey, and I were the first BSC members. (Kristy, of course, is president.) Before long we were getting tons of business. That's how Kristy views us — as a business. It was her idea to have officers, dues, a notebook, and a record book. She even made sure we put up fliers in public places to advertise ourselves.

Soon we expanded to nine members. When Dawn left, Kristy was afraid we wouldn't have enough sitters to go around. But so far, we've managed nicely.

Now you know everything about the club, and *almost* everything about Kristy. What you don't know is how Kristy ended up in such a wealthy neighborhood. It is the *most* romantic story. (Well, next to the story about my dad and Sharon.) One day, poor, overworked Mrs.

Thomas fell madly in love with a tall, dark stranger named Watson Brewer. Actually, he's medium-height, fair, and balding, but he was a nice guy and a widower. And a millionaire. *And* he fell in love back. They got married, and it was 'bye-'bye Bradford Court, hello mansion!

Yes, mansion. But don't think of drafty hallways and Lurch-like butlers. It *teems* with life. And not just the four Thomas kids. On alternate months, Watson's two kids from his previous marriage live there, too. Plus Emily Michelle, an adorable two-year-old Vietnamese girl Watson and Mrs. Thomas adopted. *Plus* Kristy's grandmother, who helps take care of Emily Michelle.

Oh, and a number of pets.

Rrrring!

"Hello, Baby-sitters Club!" Claudia said, snatching up the receiver. "Oh, hi, Mrs. Barrett. . . . Okay, can I call you back? Thanks." She hung up and announced, "This Saturday afternoon?"

I looked in the record book. "Let's see, that's a busy day. . . . Jessi's free . . . so's Kristy . . ."

"Oh! I forgot to tell you," Jessi said. "My mom's taking me to an ABT performance that day."

"Abie *who*?" Kristy asked.

Jessi giggled. "*T*. American Ballet Theater."

"Cool," said Kristy's mouth, while her eyes said *ho-hum*. "I'll do the job, as long as the DeWitt kids aren't there."

We all laughed. Mrs. Barrett is Buddy's mom. When she and Mr. DeWitt announced their engagement, their kids immediately declared war on each other. Sitting for them was a nightmare. Fortunately they've been behaving better lately, but with kids, you never know.

Jessi had a big smile on her face. I don't know whether she was happier about seeing the ABT or missing the Barrett job.

Just kidding. Jessi loves baby-sitting. If anything, she wishes she could take *more* jobs. But her parents are strict with curfews, so she can't work on weeknights.

Neither can Mal. Which is why she and Jessi are our junior members. (But don't ever talk to them about their curfews. They're *convinced* their parents treat them like babies.) Those two have so much in common. They're both horse-crazy. They love to read. Each is the oldest kid in her family. And each has a creative talent. Mal's not a trained dancer like Jessi, but you should see the stories she writes and illustrates. She's fantastic, and she wants to make it a career someday.

Two things they *don't* have in common are appearance and family size. Jessi is black, with long, elegant legs, and hair pulled straight back. Mal is white, with curly red hair, and braces. Jessi has two siblings, an eight-year-old sister named Becca and a toddler brother named Squirt. And that, as you know, is five fewer siblings than Mal has. (Yikes!)

". . . So I had to convince Jamie it was okay to go trick-or-treating," Stacey was telling everyone. "He *hated* last Halloween. He went as Peter Pan, but almost every single neighbor opened the door and said, 'Oh, look, Robin Hood!' It broke his heart."

We all groaned in sympathy.

"Anyway, I convinced him," Stacey continued. "But now I'm not sure it was a good idea. He wants to go as a shopping bag this year."

"What?" Claudia and Kristy exclaimed together.

"This way, he thinks people can just put the candy straight into his mouth," Stacey explained.

"Makes sense to me," Claudia said.

"It *would*," Kristy muttered.

"I heard that!" Claudia shot back.

Rrrrrring!

Saved by the bell.

"Hello, Baby-sitters Club!" Claudia said. "Sure, Mrs. Kuhn. I'll confer with my cohorts and call you right back!"

When Claudia hung up, Kristy practically

exploded with laughter. *"Confer with your cohorts?"* she said.

Claudia shrugged. "It sounds professional to me. Ms. Secretary, may I be appraised of the availability of . . . available sitters for Friday afternoon?"

Now everyone was giggling. I could barely keep a straight face. "Um . . . I can take that job," I managed to say.

"Nice to know *someone* takes this work seriously," Claudia said, picking up the receiver with an indignant "Hmmph."

That just made everybody laugh harder. Claudia tried to look annoyed.

Finally she gave in. She put down the phone and cracked up.

One thing about extreme happiness. It's contagious.

CHAPTER 3

"What's that?" Laurel Kuhn asked, looking up from a pile of paper dolls she had just cut out.

Her sister, Patsy, muttered, "A baseball bat." She was carefully guiding her scissors around a huge brown blob on a piece of paper.

"But it's bigger than the doll!"

"So? She's strong."

Laurel snickered. (She's six, and she's convinced she's *much* more mature than Patsy, who's five.)

When I next looked up, Laurel was drawing something that looked like an enormous green turtle. "What are *you* making?" I asked.

"A helmet," Patsy answered. "You know, in case the doll throws the bat by mistake."

"Oh."

Of course. I should have known.

I adore the Kuhn kids. All three of them are

so easy to sit for. That afternoon I only had the girls, because Jake had gotten permission to go to Buddy Barrett's house.

I noticed the pile of "clothes" the girls had cut out for their dolls — paper jeans, sweat shirts, caps, and sneakers. Not a frilly dress in sight.

Too bad Kristy wasn't there. She'd have loved it!

Kristy coaches the three Kuhn kids in softball. Their team is called Kristy's Krushers, and it's made up of kids too young (or too shy, or too uncoordinated) for T-ball or Little League. Their season had ended months ago. I guess Patsy and Laurel were already looking forward to the next one.

As the girls cut and colored on the den floor, I sat cross-legged on the sofa and breathed in the crisp air that was gusting through the window. I felt so contented. The week had breezed by. I had aced a math test and a book report, and had even enjoyed about six minutes of a gym class. What's more, I had no homework. And I was going out that night with Logan.

What a life.

I picked up a magazine and began reading.
Ka-boom!
The noise made me drop the magazine. Pat-

sy's and Laurel's heads snapped upward in surprise. It sounded as if a rhinoceros had fallen onto the house.

"What was that?" I asked.

"The front door?" Patsy guessed.

"I'll check," I said, running out of the den. I got as far as the kitchen when I ran into Jake.

Or rather, he ran into me.

"Oh!" I exclaimed. "You're back."

Jake didn't look at me. Instead he slipped by and stomped up the stairs. "I *hate* him!"

"Who?" I asked. "Buddy?"

"No," Jake shouted, "*Cruddy*! That's his *real* name!"

He ran into his bedroom and slammed the door. "*Bloody!*" his voice blurted out, muffled. *"That's what he'll be when I punch his nose!"*

Patsy and Laurel looked dumbfounded. "Did Jake punch Buddy?" Laurel asked.

"I don't think so," I said.

Jake was now tromping around his room, muttering to himself.

Whoa. This sure didn't seem like the quiet, sensitive Jake I knew.

I could tell the girls were worried. I gave them a smile and said, "Let's give him a little time to cool off. He and Buddy probably had an argument or something."

"Maybe he'd like to see our dolls," Patsy suggested.

"Uh, I don't think so," Laurel replied, pulling Patsy back toward the den. "Come on, let's finish."

I waited in the kitchen. Jake's angry pacing soon stopped. I gave him a few more moments, then went upstairs and knocked on his door.

"Yeah?" he called from inside.

"Can I come in?" I asked.

"Ooommrrr," or something like it, was the response.

"Excuse me?"

"I SAID, all right!"

I turned the knob and entered. The first thing I saw was Jake's backpack and jacket on the floor in a heap.

Jake was sitting on his bed. His eyes were red and his bedspread was rumpled all the way up to the headboard. It looked as if he'd been crying into his pillow.

I felt so bad for him. "Something really terrible happened, huh?" I asked, sitting on the edge of the bed.

Jake sniffled and looked out his window, as if I weren't in the room.

One thing about being a BSC member, you learn patience. Especially with angry kids. I was determined not to push him.

"Boy, you look furious," I said gently.

Jake exhaled loudly.

The ticking of his alarm clock seemed to be getting louder and louder.

"You guys fought about something, huh?" I finally asked.

"Yeah," Jake mumbled.

"Can you tell me what happened?"

Tick. Tick. Tick. Tick.

I moved to get up from the bed. "Well, I'll come back if — "

"I'm never going to talk to him again!" Jake blurted out. His eyes were moistening now.

"Jake," I said softly. "It's okay. You can tell me."

Sniff, sniff. Jake wiped away two tears. In a teeny voice, he said, "He invited me to his mom's wedding."

I couldn't have heard that right. He must have said *didn't invite*.

I leaned closer. "Well, maybe it's a small ceremony," I suggested. "Maybe his mom isn't going to allow kids."

Jake looked at me as if I had lost my mind. "I'm a kid."

"Well, I know — but — " I took a deep breath. "Wait. What did you just tell me?"

"Buddy . . . invited me . . . to . . . his mom's . . . wedding." He sounded as if he were explaining something to a class of Norwegians learning English.

"Oh. That's great. Why are you mad?"

Jake glowered at me, then went back to staring out the window. "You wouldn't understand."

"Try me, Jake. Really. I'm not as dumb as I look."

Oops. A smile was beginning to form.

"I just don't want to go," he replied. "Weddings are stupid."

"I see. I'll bet you said that to Buddy, and that was why he got mad, huh?"

Jake nodded.

"Well, that's all right," I assured him. "You can always call him back and — "

"No way! He thinks he's so great and he's *not*! Who cares about ugly old Franklinstein and his ugly kids anyway?"

Uh-oh. I had a feeling I knew what was going on.

By "Franklinstein," Jake meant Franklin DeWitt, Mrs. Barrett's boyfriend. Jake had always liked him.

But that was before Franklin was going to be Buddy's stepdad.

I took a deep breath and looked around Jake's room. On his desk was a framed photo of him and his dad. They were each wearing Mickey Mouse ears and eating cotton candy. Mr. Kuhn had a clump of it on his nose, and Jake was laughing hysterically. They looked so happy.

"How's your dad?" I asked.

"Okay, I guess."

"Is he coming out to visit?"

Jake began fiddling with his bedspread. "Maybe at Thanksgiving. He was supposed to come last week. But he had too much work."

"I guess it's hard to see your best friend getting a new dad," I said.

Jake's eyes blazed. "I don't want a *new* dad!"

"I know you don't, Jake."

"Buddy says Franklin is just as cool as his own dad. So he's going to have two — one that's far away and one that lives with him every day." Jake's lips were quivering now. "That is so unfair!"

He fell onto the bed and buried his face in his pillow, sobbing.

I wiped away my own tears. Poor Jake. Did his dad know how hurt Jake had been? If I were Mr. Kuhn, I'd get on the next plane.

Divorce must be so hard.

"Jake," I said gently after he stopped crying, "I know how you feel."

"You do not. You have a mom *and* dad."

"I have a stepmom. But she married my dad when I was twelve. I never knew my real mom. She died when I was a baby."

Jake sat up. "Really?"

I nodded. "I used to think everybody else's life was perfect. But you know what? No one's is."

"Oh, yeah?" grumped Jake. "*Buddy*'s is. He's also getting brothers. He's not going to have a house full of just *girls* anymore."

"Look, the Barrett kids don't always get along with the DeWitts, remember? And now they'll all be living under the same roof, sharing the bathroom, finishing each other's favorite cereals, wanting to watch different videos at the same time. Plus Buddy'll have to move out of his house. Besides, it's not so easy to have a new parent take the place of someone you love. How would you feel if your mom decided to remarry?"

"She wouldn't do that!" Jake snapped.

You never know, I wanted to say. But I didn't. I could tell Jake was thinking that very thing.

He gazed gloomily at his wall for a few moments. "I told Buddy he was my mortal enemy. Now I can't be friends with him."

"Well, I'm sure if you guys talked it out — "

"I called him Cruddy Carrot, instead of Buddy Barrett. And he called me . . ." He lowered his eyes. ". . . Fake Prune."

He looked so embarrassed and guilty. I tried not to laugh.

"If you want, I can call his house for you," I suggested.

"Oh, I'll do it," he said with a sigh, sliding off the bed. "He's *my* friend."

He shuffled out of the bedroom. I couldn't

help but overhear his conversation, which went exactly like this: "Hi, can Buddy come over? . . . Okay. . . . Hi, Buddy. You can? . . . Okay." *Click.*

Oh, well, I guess Buddy hadn't been so devastated after all.

Buddy did come over. Jake apologized, and then Buddy did, too.

I didn't think Jake would actually *admit* he was jealous. But he did. Sort of. What he said was, "I was mad because I thought you were, like, bragging or something. About your dad. Now I know it's no big deal."

Buddy looked a little confused. Then he asked, "So are you going to come to the wedding?"

"Yeah, I guess," Jake replied.

"All *riiiiight!*" Buddy exclaimed.

A peal of laughter rang out from the den. "Look!" Laurel cried out. "Patsy made a *bra!*"

Buddy glanced at Jake. Jake glanced at Buddy. They both looked as if they'd bitten into a sweat sock.

"Let's get out of here," Buddy said.

They disappeared into the backyard. A few minutes later, I heard the imitations of lasers, spacecraft, and intergalactic creatures.

And luckily for me, it stayed that way until Mrs. Kuhn returned.

CHAPTER 4

"**W**hat are you so happy about?"

Logan asked that question as we slid into a booth at the Pizza Express. Boy, were we lucky to get a booth. It was Friday night, and the place was crowded with kids from SMS and Stoneybrook High School.

"I don't know," I said with a shrug. "No reason."

Logan's smile disappeared. "Oh. It has nothing to do with me, huh?"

"No! I mean, it doesn't *not*. I mean — "

"Doesn't not?" Logan burst out laughing. "Speak English much?"

"Stop!" Now I was laughing. Logan loves to tease, but somehow it's impossible to be mad at him. (Well, almost impossible. We *have* had our disagreements.)

"I don't know," I continued. "I've just been feeling good lately, about everything. You look pretty happy yourself."

"I'm thinking about sausage and pepperoni," he replied, staring at a menu.

"That's all?" I said with a raised eyebrow.

"No." Logan looked at me with those warm, tingly, smiling eyes. "I'm also thinking about something much more important."

"Mm. What's that?"

"Extra cheese."

"Ooooh." I smacked him with the menu.

"Truce!" Logan shouted, covering his face.

"I'm sorry, this is a violence-free zone," said a voice above us.

I looked up at the waitress and felt myself blushing. "Sorry," I began.

"I can put anchovies on his half if you want," she said with a mischievous smile.

"And bean curd," I added.

"Okay, okay! I'll behave!" Logan pleaded.

We finally settled on half mushrooms, half pepperoni and extra cheese.

The waitress brought us sodas first, and Logan and I sat back on the soft seats and began to chat.

"I'm feeling pretty good, too," Logan admitted. "Coach Mills said my passing has improved so much, he might consider making me backup quarterback."

"Wow, that's fantastic!" To be honest, I don't know a quarterback from an outfielder, but it sounded important.

"Well, King heard the coach say that, and suddenly he started acting friendly," Logan continued. "Not because he's turned into a human being, but because he wants to make sure I'll pass to him."

"Figures," I said.

Clarence King is the kind of guy who thinks the idea of a *boy* baby-sitter is hilarious. He gives Logan incredible grief about being a BSC member.

We talked some more about Logan's week. Then I began telling him about my job at the Kuhns' that day. He listened carefully, sipping his soda.

"Too bad Mr. Kuhn cancelled that visit," Logan said. "Sounds like Jake really misses him."

"Well, Mr. Kuhn tries hard," I replied. "He calls a lot, writes letters and stuff — "

"Yeah, but Jake's only eight. And he's not the most confident kid to begin with. He doesn't totally understand. I mean, if *he* had plans to visit his dad, he wouldn't dream of cancelling them. He probably thinks his dad's losing interest in him."

You can see why I like Logan. He understands kids really well. (Well, that's *one* reason I like him.)

"And then this thing happens with Buddy," I added. "For a long time, *Buddy* was the one who had no dad in the house. Just a mom and two younger sisters. Now it's as if he and Jake switched places."

Logan shook his head. "No boy should have to live in a house full of girls. Pure torture."

"Very funny."

"You know what I mean. What's Jake going to do around the house, play with paper dolls? He needs . . . you know, someone like him. Someone there, who he can see. A guy."

"Like a role model."

"Exactly."

We were interrupted by a bubbling hot plate of pizza. The waitress lowered it carefully onto our table. It smelled wonderful.

End of conversation. For the next few minutes we ate silently.

But my mind was still mulling over what Logan had said.

Finally, when my stomach began begging me to stop, I said, "Logan, I was thinking. About this role model stuff. Jake's mom has been really busy lately, and she's been needing a lot of sitters. . . ."

"Mary Anne, you know I can't do much sitting these days," Logan said, "what with football practice and — "

"That's not what I mean. Mrs. Kuhn likes girl sitters anyway, because of Patsy and Laurel. But in a way, that's the problem. Don't you see?"

He didn't.

"Maybe you can come over while I'm sitting sometime. You know, throw a football around with Jake, ride bikes, whatever."

"I don't know, Mary Anne. I don't have a whole lot of time."

"Just a *little* time, then. You could drop by for an hour or so after practice. Think of how much it would mean to Jake."

Logan shrugged. "Yeah. I guess. Why not?" He looked longingly at the pizza. "Are you having any more?"

"Logan Bruno, I can't believe you are still hungry."

"I'm not. I just don't want it to go to waste."

Logan practically inhaled a pepperoni slice, then dug into another. You would think he hadn't seen food in weeks. I don't know where he puts it.

"Mary Anne, Logan! Hi!" a familiar voice called out.

I turned to see Stacey walking in with her boyfriend, Robert Brewster. "Hi!" I said, moving over.

I had to do a double take. They looked sensational. Stacey was wearing this stunning black double-breasted tuxedo-style suit with a satiny white tank underneath. Robert was wearing a navy jacket with a tie and crisp gray wool pants.

Not exactly your average Pizza Express attire.

Robert and Stacey sat right down, grinning from ear to ear. Before I could say a thing about their clothes, Robert said, "Let's order. We're starving."

Logan pointed to the one remaining slice, now cold and lying in a puddle of grease. "Help yourself."

"Hey, thanks." Robert picked it up and jammed it into his mouth.

I did not get sick. Somehow.

"You guys would not believe where we've been," Stacey said.

"Shoomee," Robert commented with a mouthful of coagulated pizza.

"Chez Maurice," Stacey translated. "With Wayne McConville and Kathleen Lopez."

(Wayne is a friend of Robert's on the basketball team. I don't know Kathleen well, but I remember she tried out for the cheerleading squad back when Stacey did.)

No wonder Stacey and Robert were so dressed. Chez Maurice is the fanciest restaurant in Stoneybrook. "So what are you doing *here*?" I asked.

"Well, see, at Chez Maurice we're giving

our waiter the order," Stacey began, "and Wayne announces, 'I'll have sweetbreads.' We all look at him, and he says, 'Hey, I'm in the mood for something sweet.' Like he orders it all the time."

Robert was gagging, trying not to laugh.

"Well, as we're finishing our salads, the waiter brings the entrees," Stacey went on. "And Wayne's looks absolutely disgusting. It's, like, *grayish-white*! So Wayne asks what it is. And the waiter says, 'The thymus gland of a calf.' "

I could feel the mushrooms dancing around in my stomach. Logan moaned.

"Wayne turned *green*," Robert continued. "No one could eat. We paid up and booked. When the waiter asked if he could put the food in a doggy bag, Wayne said he didn't have a dog. Anyway, we just walked around town, hanging out. When Mr. McConville picked us up, we told him dinner was great. We were too embarrassed to admit what had happened."

"So here we are," Stacey said.

"Wayne said he had to go home and rest," Robert added.

"Can I help you?" the Pizza Express waitress asked with a sly smile. "Filet mignon? Caviar?"

Robert began, "Do you have sweet — "

"Don't!" Stacey cut in. "A small plain pizza, please."

Logan and I ordered dishes of ice cream.

Before long we were all pigging out, *howling* as Robert and Stacey went into more and more gruesome detail.

By the time we all finished, I could barely move. It had been a fun night.

As we went outside and breathed in the cool air, a voice called out, "Hey, guys!"

Two people approached us. Can you guess who they were? I'll give you a hint: they were dying with hunger.

Yup. Wayne and Kathleen.

Without saying a word, we all burst out laughing. People on the sidewalk were staring at us.

But we didn't care a bit.

I was still smiling when I got home. But I could not go straight to bed. One vital thing was missing, one thing that would make the day perfect.

It was ten o'clock, which meant seven o'clock California time.

I went to the kitchen phone and called Dawn.

"Hello?" I was in luck! Dawn's voice.

"Dawn? Hi, it's me!"

"Mary Anne! Hi! I was just thinking about you. We just got back from this cookout at the

beach. What a disaster! I brought along some tempeh to grill, but it fell into the coals — and some cute guy insisted I have one of his *hot dogs*! I said, 'Yuck! Pig carcasses and carcinogens!' The words just, like, flew out of my mouth. I thought I would die!"

For about a half hour we traded food stories, giggling like crazy. It felt soooo good to talk to her.

I went to bed that night with a huge smile on my face.

CHAPTER 5

Saturday

Today I sat for the Barrett kids.
Well, it started out that way. A few guests wandered over, too. Like the Kuhns. And Marilyn and Carolyn and Matt and Haley. And a few Pikes.

But that was cool. No big deal. It was good to see familiar, happy faces.

Ha! Little did I suspect the warped and twisted minds that lurked within them all . . . .

Kristy was being dramatic. Actually, the first part of her entry was true. She's terrific with large groups of kids. She doesn't mind if the whole neighborhood wanders over. To her, it just means bigger teams.

You already know the Kuhn kids and Buddy Barrett. Buddy has two younger sisters — Suzi (who's five) and Marnie (two). Marilyn and Carolyn Arnold are eight-year-old twins. Haley Braddock is nine and her brother Matt is seven (Matt is profoundly deaf and communicates using sign language). And three Pike kids were there: Vanessa (nine), Nicky (eight), and Margo (seven).

"Okay, red team line up next to the garage!" Kristy called out, holding a red kickball. "That means Haley, Nicky, Marilyn, Carolyn, Suzi, and Jake!"

All of them rushed over to the garage, squealing — except Nicky Pike. He looked up at Kristy, distressed. "Red is a girls' color!" Nicky said.

"Nickyyyyy, come on," Kristy pleaded.

"Can't you give us a different name?"

Kristy's idea factory went to work. "Okay. Since it's Halloween, Vampires versus Ghosts! Vampires up first."

"We're the Vampires!" Nicky shouted, running to his team.

"Boooooo!" wailed Marnie, holding her arms out and rocking back and forth.

Buddy, Patsy, Laurel, Vanessa, Margo, and Matt took the field. Kristy had to convince Marnie she was too young to play, which she did by sitting Marnie in front of a huge toy backhoe (her latest obsession).

Kristy marked off bases (a tree stump, a fence post, a crack in the driveway, and a bald patch in the grass) and announced that the oldest on each team would pitch.

Vanessa took the ball and Nicky stepped up to the bald patch. "I going to suck your bloooood!" he said in a Dracula voice.

"I'm going to hit your head," Vanessa replied, rearing back as if to throw the ball.

Kristy calmed them down. Then she helped Marnie, who was trying to lift a brick with her backhoe.

Then she helped Margo, who hurt her foot by kicking the dirt instead of the ball.

Then she had to rescue Suzi because Nicky was holding a daddy longlegs and threatening to put it in her hair.

Eventually things settled down. Kristy played for awhile with Marnie, then took her inside to change her diaper.

When she returned, she noticed Buddy and Jake were missing.

"Where are Buddy and Jake?" she called out.

"I don't know," a chorus of voices answered.

Crasssh!

The sound came from the bathroom window, just around the corner of the house.

Kristy ran to the window and asked, "What's going on in there?"

"Nothing!" Buddy's voice called back.

As she began to walk away, she heard Jake saying, "Ew, it's all dusty!"

"Wipe it up with wet toilet paper," Buddy replied. "Hurry up!"

Mischief Alert.

Kristy went straight for the back door. But as she stepped inside, Buddy came racing through the kitchen. His face was streaked with red marks.

"Aaaaagh!" he screamed, clutching his throat.

"Buddy? Are you — ?"

Buddy raced past Kristy and went outside. "Aaaaagh!" he repeated.

Now Jake appeared. He had on a black Batman cape, turned inside out so the bat symbol didn't show. His face was powdered pale white, and his eyes were circled with black eyeshadow. He had darkened his eyebrows with makeup and made them meet, so it looked as if he had one long brow across his forehead.

When he smiled at Kristy, plastic fangs jutted out of his mouth. "Greeeetings," he said sinisterly.

"I don't believe this." All Kristy could think of was how Mrs. Barrett would look when she noticed her makeup messed up.

Outside, the kickball game had completely dissolved. Everyone was shrieking and laughing and running wild. Kristy ran out. Behind her, Jake was bellowing, "I shall get every one of you!"

Carolyn picked up two sticks, crossed them, and ran toward Jake. "You have to die now!" she announced.

Buddy was lying on the ground, pretending to be dead. He had drawn two red lipstick marks on his neck, like bites.

Poor little Marnie couldn't handle her brother's death scene. She was sobbing like crazy, her fingers shoved in her mouth.

Kristy scooped her up and let out one of her patented whistles. (It's more like a siren.) "Okay, I want Vampires and Ghosts over by the picnic table — *on the double.*"

Zoom. They became the quietest, most obedient kids on earth.

"Now, I guess you guys are more interested

in scaring each other than playing — "

"We'll play," Marilyn insisted.

"Do we have to go home?" Margo asked.

"No, no. I have a better idea," Kristy said. "Since Halloween's so close, how about doing a Halloween project? You could plan what costumes to wear, how you're going to decorate your house — "

"I'll get some makeup!" Suzi announced.

"No makeup!" Kristy said hastily.

"Buddy and Jake used it," Suzi protested.

"Yes, and they're both going to explain that to your mom," Kristy said.

"Uh-oh," Laurel muttered.

Haley had been signing Kristy's sentences to Matt. Now his fingers were flying in response.

"Matt says he wants to be a pirate," Haley said.

"Me too!" Nicky piped up. "I can be Captain Hook and he'll be Mr. Smee!"

Matt began signing furiously. "He's Hook and you're Smee," Haley said. "Smee's too fat."

"Hey!" Nicky cried.

"Fatso!" Vanessa taunted.

"Guys!" Kristy warned.

Patsy blurted out, "I know! I'll put cobwebs all over the front door, to scare kids away!"

"Then we can have all the candy," Laurel added.

"I'm going to hide inside the door and scare the trick-or-treaters," Buddy said.

"You'll be trick-or-treating *yourself!*" Suzi reminded him.

"Oh, yeah," Buddy mumbled.

"Duh," Vanessa said.

"Forget the cobwebs," Jake barged in. "I think we should make a haunted house!"

Nicky snickered. "Yeah, right."

"I mean it," Jake insisted. "Like, in somebody's basement or attic. We could sell tickets."

"What a good idea," Kristy remarked. She was impressed. That was the kind of thing she would think of (especially the ticket-selling part).

"We could all dress in scary costumes and hide in the shadows," Buddy said. "Then . . . *BOO-AH-HAH-HAH-HAH!*"

Marnie burst into tears. "No more," she told Buddy.

By now the kids had divided themselves into two groups. The Arnold twins were still gabbing about costumes with Suzi, Patsy, Laurel, and Margo.

The rest — Jake, Buddy, Nicky, Vanessa, Matt, and Haley — were bursting with excitement about the haunted house.

"We could have a black light — you know, it only lights up certain things in the dark," Vanessa suggested. "My dad has one."

"We just got a new refrigerator!" Haley blurted out eagerly.

"Uh-huh," Nicky said dryly. "We're all so happy to hear that."

"The box!" Haley barged on. "We can use it as a coffin!"

Vanessa shivered. "Oooooooh, spooky!"

"We can have slimy stuff hanging over everybody's head," Buddy said.

"And, like, fake body parts on the floor," Jake offered. "And a witch can run around slipping on them."

"That's not *scary*," Vanessa said. "The witch should, like, pick them up and eat them."

Nicky made a face. "Gross!"

"They won't be *real*," Vanessa snapped.

"Matt says we should put up signs around the neighborhood," Haley said.

"Yeah! With the address and ticket price," Vanessa chimed in.

"What address?" Buddy asked.

"Here," Jake said. "My mom wouldn't mind."

"How much should we charge?" Haley asked.

"Ten dollars," Buddy suggested.

"A quarter!" Nicky said.

"A bar of candy," was Vanessa's idea.

"Tandy! Tandy!" Marnie started squealing.

Whoops. "How about an apple?" Kristy asked her.

"Appo."

Kristy brought Marnie inside. But it took some effort. Kristy was dying to jump in with suggestions about the haunted house.

But she never did. The kids were doing just fine by themselves.

It promised to be a wild Halloween.

CHAPTER 6

When I showed up at the Kuhns' house that Tuesday, Patsy came to the door with a skull.

"Hi, Mary Anne," she said with a scratchy voice. "My name's Herman. I'm *dying* to see you. Get it?"

Giggling, she ran back into the den, shouting, "Mary Anne's here!"

Mrs. Kuhn walked in, all bundled up and ready to leave. "Hi, Mary Anne. The girls have a skeleton-building kit. Maybe you can help them, or get Jake to. It's a little above their age level."

"Sure," I said.

"You know where the snacks are. I'll be back way before dinner. 'Bye."

" 'Bye."

She went out the front door, and I walked back to the den.

"No, silly, that's the *left* hand!" Laurel was saying.

On the floor in front of them was a large box full of plastic bones. Patsy and Laurel had attached the head to the neck bone, the right arm to the shoulder blade — and the left hand to the right arm.

Patsy took off the hand and snapped on a foot.

"Noooo!" Laurel rolled on the floor, giggling.

Patsy then placed a hip bone on the skull's head. "Like my hat?" she said.

Now Laurel and I were both laughing.

"What's *that*?"

We looked up to see Jake in the doorway, scowling.

"Herman," Laurel answered. "Our skeleton. Come on, help us."

"No way," Jake mumbled.

"I don't know, Jake," I said. "They've got Herman's foot on his arm and he's eating his hips."

I thought the *fun* aspect might appeal to him. He looked as if I'd just offered him turnip soup.

"I finished my homework," he said. "I'll be outside."

He slunk away. I sat with the girls, watching them make a mutant human being. After awhile they began actually figuring out the correct bone positions.

I left them as they pondered a calf bone.

Whap!

Whap!

The dull noises floated into the kitchen from outside. I looked out the back window. Jake was kicking a soccer ball against the garage wall.

I sat at the kitchen table and began doing some homework. The front doorbell rang before I got very far.

I ran and opened it.

"Hey, can Jake come out to play?"

It was Logan. His cleats were slung over his shoulder, along with his backpack. He was sweaty, gross, and filthy. But he had that dimply, melt-your-heart smile, so I hardly noticed the other stuff.

"Hi! You made it!" I said.

"I ran over from practice. I figured you'd still be here."

"Great! I'm so glad you came. Jake's out back."

Logan walked through the house and went out the back door. "Hey, Jakey!" he called out. "What's up?"

Jake looked up quizzically. "What are you doing here?" he asked.

"Just stopped by to say hi. Nice ball." He picked up the soccer ball, spun it on his finger, and tossed it at Jake's feet. "See if you can get it by me."

Logan ran to the garage and stood in front of the open door, legs apart.

Jake grinned. He began kicking the ball, running toward Logan. When he was a few feet in front of the door, he gave the ball a hard kick.

Logan caught it easily. "Aww, right at me! Don't forget rule number one: kick it where they ain't! Now come on, try again. This time draw me away from the center, then kick it into the place I left open."

Jake nodded enthusiastically and went back to try again.

Logan gave me a wink. I gave him a thumbs-up and went back inside.

In the living room, Herman's feet were all set to walk in opposite directions.

"I think the hip's wrong," Laurel said.

I helped them out a bit. Then Patsy insisted on making Herman some outfits.

How do you clothe a skeleton? This was really a job for a fashion expert, like Claudia or Stacey. But I tried. We measured Herman and began making some patterns.

"*Score!*" shouted Logan and Jake outside. Then I could hear Jake whooping with triumph.

I smiled. I hadn't heard Jake so happy in a long time.

Inside, however, life with Herman was becoming even weirder. He was a difficult fit. And he looked ridiculous in paper pants and a shirt.

The girls found the whole thing hilarious. When he was fully dressed, they stood him up on a plastic stand that had been included in the kit.

Patsy took a Barbie from a toy box. "La la la la," she sang, making the Barbie walk toward Herman. "Excuse me, sir, do you have the time? *Eeeeeek!*"

Laurel went rummaging around and came up with a few dolls and hand puppets.

The Herman Show was underway. The plot went something like this: Herman scares the good people of Stoneybrook, Herman buys a hat, Herman chases Bugs Bunny and rips his pants.

Herman was being stalked by GI Joe when Logan and Jake appeared at the door. They were both panting and red-faced. Jake had this humongous smile.

"Hey, guys," Logan said.

"I beat him one-on-one," Jake announced.

Logan winked. "This kid is dangerous. Well, I have to go."

"One more game?" Jake pleaded.

"Sorry, Jakey. I have to save my energy for next time."

"Oh, all right," Jake said. "Can you come over tomorrow?"

Jake walked Logan to the door. I could hear the two of them chattering away happily.

"He *hates* when people call him Jakey," Laurel remarked.

I smiled. "Not anymore."

I heard the front door close, and a moment later Jake came back into the room. He looked at Herman and laughed. "What did you do to him?"

"We're making a show!" Patsy said.

Jake took a plastic witch out of the toy box. "Hey, handsome," he said to Herman in a crackly voice. "Wanna fly with me?"

The Old Jake was returning. Thanks to Logan.

And me.

I mean, it *was* my idea.

Mrs. Kuhn returned home late, minutes after my dad had called, wondering where I was. "I'm so sorry," she apologized, fumbling in her purse for money to pay me.

"That's okay," I said. "Everything went great."

"Good. Now before you go, let me give you

some more dates when I'll need a sitter."

She took out a calendar and I wrote down the information.

We said a quick good-bye, and Mrs. Kuhn scooted into the den. The kids were still in the midst of The Herman Show. "Sit and watch, Mom!" Jake urged her.

I could hear Mrs. Kuhn's surprised laughter as I headed outside. It was a beautiful sound.

CHAPTER 7

Mrs. Kuhn was thrilled. She called the BSC the next day to say so. She requested me for three afternoon jobs the next week, on Monday, Thursday, and Friday.

I mentioned that to Logan later on. His response was, "Good, Jake owes me a rematch!"

He was being so sweet.

Anyway, he didn't exactly *promise* he'd return for any of those jobs. But he said he'd try.

So I was happy when Jake and I answered the Kuhns' doorbell on Monday and discovered Logan there.

Jake's face lit up like a jack-o'-lantern. "I didn't know *you* were coming over!" he said.

"You think I would let you get away with beating me last week?" Logan replied. "This time I'm going to whup you."

"Oh, yeah?" Jake said.

He ran through the house, with Logan behind him.

I went into the den and began reading to the girls from *The Lion, the Witch, and the Wardrobe*. I couldn't hear exactly what happened outside, but Logan described it to me later.

According to Logan, Jake is not a natural athlete. But Logan also believes *anyone* can do well at sports; all it takes is learning the rules, practicing, and having confidence. (At least that's what he tells me. Personally, I don't believe it.)

Anyway, Jake was improving, compared to the week before. He eagerly took Logan's suggestions and didn't seem as afraid as he had been.

After a half hour they went in and got some juice from the fridge. As they walked back outside, Jake asked, "Are you going to be a pro soccer player?"

Logan laughed. "No. I'm not *that* good."

"You're a great coach. I wish you coached the Stars."

"The Stars? I didn't know you were on a team."

"Yeah. In Saturday soccer league."

"What position?"

Jake shrugged. "I just go where they tell me. Nobody ever kicks the ball to me, except Buddy sometimes. I mostly just stand around."

"Maybe I'll stop by and watch one of your games. Give you some pointers."

Jake was so excited he almost choked on his apple cider. "Great!" he finally said. "I was going to quit."

"Don't do *that*. Soccer's fun."

"That's what Buddy always tells me. But *he* has fun because he's *good*."

"Don't worry. You'll be good, too."

"Oh!" Jake suddenly blurted out. "Turn around! Don't ask why, just do it."

Logan obeyed him. He heard some shuffling and Velcro-tearing sounds. "Okay. Now."

When Logan turned back, he burst out laughing. "Jason!" he yelled.

Jake had put his plastic shin guard over his face, fastening its Velcro straps behind his head. He looked like Jason from the *Friday the Thirteenth* movies.

"Like it?" Jake was beaming when he pulled it off. "Is it scary?"

"You bet."

"I might use it in this haunted house me and my friends are making! We're going to have it in our basement. Mom can cook some spinach and put it all over me — and when it dries, it'll look like seaweed! You know, like I just came out of a swamp?"

"Disgusting!" Logan said. "I love it!"

"Or I might be a vampire. Will you come to our house? It's going to be in our basement on Halloween. With spooky music and decorations. Tickets are only twenty dollars, and — "

"Whoa. Time out. Twenty dollars! Isn't that a little high?"

Jake looked at him blankly. "High?"

"Think about the events at your school fair — you know, the moon walk, stuff like that. How much do they cost?"

"But this will be *much* better than those!"

They tossed some numbers around. Finally they settled on fifty cents.

After a few more minutes of soccer, Logan went home. On his way out he told me Jake seemed very happy.

I wasn't surprised.

Jake was still playing, by himself, when Mrs. Kuhn arrived. I could hear him yelling "Yes!" every few minutes.

"Hi, everybody!" Mrs. Kuhn called out.

"Hi!" Patsy, Laurel, and I echoed.

We were still in the den. I was in the middle of a chapter. "To be continued," I said, closing the book.

"No! No!" Patsy squealed. "You can't *do* that!"

"But your mom's home — " I began.

Mrs. Kuhn was standing in the doorway with a big smile. "That's all right. Everybody looks so happy. You go ahead and finish. I'll get Jake to help me with dinner."

I ended up reading an extra chapter. I finished at 5:19. I had exactly eleven minutes to get to the BSC meeting.

I quickly said my good-byes. As I left, Jake and Mrs. Kuhn were busy chopping vegetables. Jake was in hysterics, cutting red peppers into weird shapes and dropping them into the salad bowl.

Logan hadn't planned to show up during my Thursday job. But he did. He told me later he was really enjoying his time with Jake. He'd looked forward to that visit all day.

I guess being a role model is as much fun as having one.

Laurel and I spent most of that job helping Patsy learn to ride her bike up and down the driveway. Once in awhile I caught a glimpse of Logan and Jake. They seemed to be playing *hard*, both of them concentrating and weaving around each other.

Logan only stayed a few minutes, because he had to go shopping with his dad. Jake looked terribly disappointed about that.

But afterward I watched him kicking the ball

around by himself. Even I could see he'd improved.

On Friday, Mrs. Kuhn met me at the door with a big smile. "The kids can't wait to see you," she said. "Jake's in the backyard, *singing*! His spirits have really picked up this week — no small thanks to you!"

I blushed. "Oh, it's not me — "

"Honestly, Mary Anne, you are modest to a fault!" she said with a laugh. As she turned to leave, she added, "I'll be at a doctor's appointment. I usually have to wait a long time to see her; that's why I scheduled you for two hours. I'll call if she's running any later. Have fun!"

With that, Mrs. Kuhn ran to the car.

Patsy and Laurel were dying to play outside. As they put on their coats in the kitchen, I could see Jake in the backyard. He was dribbling a basketball in rhythm, while singing, "All day, all night, Mary Anne. . . ." in this off-key voice.

The girls barged out the door. "Oooh, Jake and Mary Anne, Jake and Mary Anne!" Laurel sang.

Jake held onto his basketball and glared at them. "It's just a *song*!"

"So's 'Jake and Mary Anne, Jake and Mary Anne!' " Laurel taunted.

"Dork face!" Jake began chasing Laurel around the yard with the basketball.

I managed to get myself between them. Jake reared back and threw. The ball sailed right toward me. I stuck my hands out to catch it.

The ball beaned me on the head and bounced away. (Do they give a prize for World's Worst Athlete?)

Let me tell you, it did not tickle. "Yeow!"

"Oops, sorry. You okay?"

I tried to ignore the ringing bells in my sore head. "Fine. But please don't do that again."

"Okay," Jake agreed. Running after the ball, he called out, "Is Logan coming?"

"I think so," I replied. "At least he said so during lunch."

"Yyyyyes!" Jake shouted, thrusting his fist in the air. "Do you know if he's a good basketball player?"

"Probably."

"Yyyyyes again!"

Well, it turns out Logan is a great basketball player. When he arrived, he proved it. Jake, Patsy, Laurel, and I watched in awe as he made baskets from a million feet away. Swish, swish, swish.

I heard "Yyyyyes!" from Jake many more times than I cared to.

You should have seen his face. He seemed so proud of Logan.

64

The girls and I played hide-and-seek while Logan gave Jake basketball tips. Once in awhile I would catch Jake tossing in a basket and shrieking with delight. Logan was so patient and encouraging. He was treating Jake like a little brother.

Before long the boys had new nicknames for each other: "Loge-man!" and "Jake-o!" (The names seemed to come with exclamation points attached to them.)

When Jake complained about tired arms, Logan lifted him onto his shoulders. "Okay, here comes Air Jake-o . . ." he announced. "He drives to the baseboard . . . pumps . . . shoots . . ."

Jake was so close to the hoop, he just flipped it right in.

"*Yyyyyes!*" they both bellowed.

"*Nnnnno!*" Patsy and Laurel shouted from behind the garbage cans.

"Found you!" I called out.

Logan and Jake fell onto the grass, laughing. Patsy and Laurel ran away from me, giggling. Why? I don't know, but I chased them around the yard anyway.

It was one of those days.

"Okay, Jake-o," I heard Logan say. "I have to hit the road."

"Ohhhhh, shoot," Jake groaned. "Stay longer."

"I can't."

"Have some juice or something."

"Oh, okay. I am thirsty."

"Me too," Laurel piped up.

"Me five!" Patsy said.

Laurel gave her a look. "What happened to three and four?"

"Don't you even *know* how *old* I am?" Patsy scolded.

We all went inside. I got the girls juice and sat next to Logan at the table.

We were gabbing away when the front door opened.

"Hello! I'm ba-ack!" Mrs. Kuhn sang out. Her keys jingled as she walked toward the kitchen. "Guess who didn't have to wait at the doc — "

She never finished her sentence. She just stopped in the kitchen doorway.

Her eyes flickered from Logan to me. Her smile tightened.

In that moment I realized I had never told her about Logan. Never asked if he could come over, either.

I hadn't thought it was a big deal. Mrs. Kuhn probably wouldn't have, either, except for two small facts.

Logan was a boy. I was a girl.

And I looked like the world's biggest sneak.

"Hi, Mommy!" Patsy screamed, running to hug Mrs. Kuhn's knees.

"Hello, sweetheart." Mrs. Kuhn gave her daughter a hug, but her eyes never left mine. "So, we have a . . . visitor?"

Logan stood up with a smile. "Hello, Mrs. Kuhn. I'm Logan Bruno," he reminded her.

"What a surprise," Mrs. Kuhn said.

"He's the *best* athlete," Jake insisted.

"Ha-ha." Logan's laugh sounded so forced. I could tell Mrs. Kuhn was making him nervous. "Jake's getting pretty good himself."

"Now, Mary Anne," Mrs. Kuhn barged on, "correct me if I'm wrong, but I don't believe we discussed anyone else coming over today."

"It's okay, Mom," Jake chimed in. "Logan's been here before."

"*Has* he?" she asked.

"Sure. He's Mary Anne's boyfriend."

Ugh.

I felt as if someone had pulled a drawstring around my stomach.

"Uh, well, it's been nice!" Logan blurted out. "See you!"

He left so fast I could feel a breeze.

The kids were slurping the bottoms of their juice glasses with straws. They didn't seem to notice anything was wrong.

"Will you three please go into the den while

I talk to Mary Anne?" Mrs. Kuhn said firmly.

As they left, my eyes began to water. I *hate* confrontations.

"Do you . . . *often* invite your boyfriend over when you sit?" Mrs. Kuhn asked.

"No," I said.

My mind was racing. What was I supposed to tell her next? That I thought Jake needed a strong male figure in his life?

That was the truth. It was what I *wanted* to say.

But how would that make her feel? It would be like *criticizing* her. Telling her she wasn't doing enough. Not being a good enough parent.

Years ago my dad had gone through that. My grandparents doubted he could be a single parent. I know how much it hurt his feelings.

I couldn't say it. I just stared at the tabletop and said, "I'm sorry, Mrs. Kuhn. It won't happen again."

She didn't scream. She didn't scold me. She didn't refuse to pay me. She didn't do much of anything. She just led me to the door and said good-bye.

But as I left the house, I felt numb.

I ran to the Baby-sitters Club meeting. I had to talk to somebody about this.

I was in major trouble.

CHAPTER 8

"**W**hat happened to *you*?" Kristy asked as I barged into Claudia's bedroom.

I was early. Only Claudia and Kristy were there. They were both looking at me as if I had a plant growing out of my forehead.

"I — I — " I was trying to keep from bursting into tears. If I did, I'd be underwater for a half hour.

Rrrrrring!

Kristy reluctantly snatched up the receiver. "Hello, Baby-sitters Club!" Her forehead crinkled right up, and she stopped staring at me. "What? She's right here, Mrs. Kuhn."

My heart dropped through the floor.

I could hear Mrs. Kuhn's voice, like a distant bird in a tin can, as she talked to Kristy. Kristy listened intently, nodding from time to time. "Uh-huh. . . . Yes, he is an associate member. . . . No, our policy is to send only the scheduled sitter, unless other arrangements are agreed on. . . . No, I had no idea . . . Well, I apologize, Mrs. Kuhn, I didn't know . . . Yes, I will talk to her . . . you can be sure . . . good-bye."

Kristy did not slam the receiver down. She just placed it quietly. I have to admire her for that.

"What was *that* all about?" she asked.

"Here," Claudia said, holding out a box of Mallomars. "You look like you could use one of these."

"No, thanks." I flopped down on the bed next to her. "I — I — "

"We heard that part already," Claudia said with a smile.

"Stop," Kristy scolded.

But Claudia's joke loosened me up just enough. The words came pouring out. "I invited Logan to come over to the Kuhns' last week. But not to see *me*. I wasn't sneaking around or anything. It was for *Jake*. I mean, he was so depressed about his dad. And his best friend was all excited about getting a *new* dad. So I felt bad for him. I just thought it might be nice if Logan came over once in awhile and did a few *boy* things with him. That's all."

"How many times did you invite Logan over?" Kristy asked.

"It wasn't . . . a *plan* like that," I said. "I

just asked him to drop by whenever he could. They both had such a good time with each other. Jake was *soooo* happy. You should have seen him."

Claudia looked puzzled. "Well, if that's all it was, why didn't you tell Mrs. Kuhn?"

"I didn't mean *not* to tell her. I guess it just didn't come up. One day *she'd* be in a hurry, or else *I* would . . ." I sighed. "But I guess in the back of my mind I was afraid to tell her. Because when she finally asked me, I couldn't. I thought she'd take it wrong — like I was trying to make up for what she couldn't give Jake. Does that make sense?"

"Yeah." Claudia nodded thoughtfully. "I can see what you mean, but still . . ."

I felt about two feet tall. And I kept shrinking as the other members walked in and Claudia explained the whole thing to them.

The worst thing was seeing the expressions on everyone's faces. Like they couldn't believe I'd done it.

Kristy called the meeting to order at 5:30. My dilemma, of course, was the first order of business.

"Look, we all know Jake's a sensitive kid," Kristy said. "And it's nice that you tried to help him. But you should have said something, Mary Anne. Right at the beginning."

"I don't think Mrs. Kuhn would have

minded," Jessi added. "She might have been glad to see Jake with a new friend."

"Especially when she saw how happy it made him," Stacey said. "I mean, that would make her life *easier*, right? Every mom wants that!"

"Besides, Logan *is* a BSC member," Kristy reminded me. "She could have hired him."

"I . . . I guess you're right," I muttered.

Kristy was trying not to look agitated. (It wasn't working.) "Think of how this looks, Mary Anne. Not just for you, but for the club. Mrs. Kuhn is angry now. You think she *isn't* going to spread this around? She's probably on the phone right now. What will the other parents think? Will they trust any of us again?"

My head was sinking. My hair was falling in front of my eyes, blocking everyone out.

Kristy was right. I had let the Baby-sitters Club down.

"I — I really blew it," I managed to squeak before the floodgates opened.

I slumped against the wall, sobbing. Claudia put her arm around me. "Hey, it's okay. We'll work it out. Right, Kristy?"

I didn't hear an answer. Of course not. The BSC was Kristy's first concern. It had to be.

What a mess. Not only was I in trouble, but the BSC's reputation was damaged, and I may have lost my very best friend in the world.

I was hoping someone would crack a joke, but everybody just waited quietly for me to calm down. Finally Kristy said, "All right, this is serious but it's not the end of the world. I think we need to figure out two things. How to make things right with Mrs. Kuhn, and how to prevent this from happening again."

"Maybe we need to draw up a statement," Shannon suggested. "You know, swearing that we'll never ask anyone over without permission. We could sign it and mail copies to our clients — "

"That's so formal," Stacey said. "I think this is, like, a one-time thing. I mean, we can see you meant well, Mary Anne. But you *did* make a mistake. I think you should write to Mrs. Kuhn, explaining everything. Or at least go over and have a talk with her. Come clean."

"I think so, too," Claudia agreed. "You can handle it, Mary Anne. You're such a nice person, she would never think you were criticizing her."

"Wait a minute, why just Mary Anne?" Kristy asked. "Logan's responsible, too. *He* should have known better."

"They could both go over," Jessi suggested.

"Isn't anybody going to talk to Logan about this?" Mallory asked.

"*I* will." Her jaw set defiantly, Kristy reached for the phone.

"Don't," I said. "I'll talk to him later."

"But this is a club matter, too," Kristy replied. "He should know how we all feel about this."

Kristy picked up the receiver and began tapping out Logan's number.

I cringed. I hoped he had gone for a long bike ride.

To a place like Pennsylvania.

"Hello, Mrs. Bruno, this is Kristy Thomas. Is Logan there? Okay, thanks."

So much for the bike ride. Logan was about to receive the Wrath of President Kristy.

"Hi, it's Kristy. . . . Yes, I *do* know about it. Mrs. Kuhn just called and she's furious. . . . No, Mary Anne didn't tell her. . . . Uh-huh, I know Jake enjoyed it. . . . I like Jake, too. But that's not the point. I'm talking about damage control."

Damage control?

"No, I'm *not* trying to sound like a police sergeant," Kristy continued. "This is serious, Logan. It could hurt the status of this club as we know it. Mrs. Kuhn's mad. She thinks you were sneaking over to be with Mary Anne. That's absolutely against the rules. . . . Well, okay, we'll *make* a rule for it to be against! The point is, you let us down. . . ."

I thought she was going to hang up on him,

but she didn't. She listened quietly for a long while.

"Yeah, I know you feel bad," she finally said. "Mary Anne does, too. I just wanted you to know how *we* all feel. Now will you write to Mrs. Kuhn or call her? . . . Okay. Here she is."

Kristy gave me the phone. "He wants to talk to you."

"Hi, Logan?" My voice sounded tiny and weak.

"Hi," Logan said. "I guess I messed things up, huh?"

"We both did," I replied.

"Sorry I left so fast. That was dumb. I should have stayed and helped you out. I guess I figured you'd straighten it out. But Kristy says you didn't tell Mrs. Kuhn the truth."

"I didn't tell her much of anything. We'll talk about it later, okay?"

"Okay. Call me when you get home."

"I will. 'Bye."

" 'Bye."

When I hung up, the room fell completely silent. It felt like a funeral home.

Claudia went over to her closet and pulled out a big bag of chips. "Hey, if we're not going to talk, we might as well eat."

I tried to smile. I took a few chips. I ate them. I didn't taste a thing.

CHAPTER 9

Saturday

Flash to the BSC newsroom. Today marks the official beginning of the first annual Stoneybrook Scare Wars. We take you, live, to correspondent Mallory Pike.

Thanks, Stacey. It started this morning as a little battle.

A skirmish.

And then it escalated.

Yes, the streets'll be rough out there this Halloween, folks. As for me, I may stay inside...

I'm glad somebody could crack a joke after Friday's meeting. I sure couldn't.

Stacey went to the Pikes' house bright and early Saturday morning to help Mallory sit for her younger siblings.

Usually sitting for the Pikes is a little like being a traffic cop. You point everyone in the right direction and try to prevent accidents.

It wasn't always like that. Long, long ago, Mal was an only child. That lasted just one year, until the triplets were born. Adam, Jordan, and Byron are ten years old now. Then came Vanessa, Nicky, Margo, and finally Claire, who's five.

I think if any more were born, the Pikes would be a town instead of a family.

On that Saturday, Mr. and Mrs. Pike had dropped Margo and Claire off at a party, then gone to a brunch.

That left five sitting charges. Two of them (Nicky and Vanessa) immediately ran to the basement, to plan their haunted house.

The triplets began tossing around a football on the front lawn.

"Aren't you going to work on the haunted house?" Stacey asked them.

Adam rolled his eyes. "No *way*. That is the world's stupidest idea."

"Why?" Mallory asked.

"Be*cause*," Jordan said as if he were explaining something to a two-year-old, "if you're running a *haunted house*, you can't *trick-or-treat*. Then you can't get *candy*."

"Oh," said Stacey and Mal.

They went into the kitchen as the triplets continued their game.

Little bursts of laughter floated up from the basement. Every few seconds, Nicky or Vanessa would cry out, "Ewwwww!"

What a job. Two happy kids in the basement. Three happy kids outside. Everything was nice and peaceful.

For about fifteen minutes.

Wham! The back door swung open and Buddy and Jake ran in. Both were dressed in soccer uniforms, and Jake was holding a full shopping bag. "Hi!" Buddy said. "We came to help plan the haunted house, then we have to go to a game."

"Our moms said it was all right," Jake insisted.

Whoosh! Down they went.

Four kids in the basement.

Then another *wham* and another *whoosh*. This time it was Haley and Matt. Their mom had said it was all right, too.

Six kids. The basement was filling up.

"*Grrrossss!*" Haley's voice shouted.

"Get that thing away from me!" Nicky said.

"Stacey! Mallory!"

"Uh-oh," Mal muttered.

"Time for some damage control," Stacey replied.

They tromped downstairs. Buddy and Jake had stretched a huge glob of plastic slime between them. They were running after the other kids, trying to trap them.

"Tell them to stop!" Haley said.

She was dressed in a flowing costume with a fake tiara on her head.

As Mal ran after the two boys, Stacey asked Haley, "Who are you?"

"Madame Leveaux," Haley replied, curtseying. "I weel be telling fortunes at zee haunted house."

Stacey recognized the outfit and the accent. Haley had been Madame Leveaux during a fund-raiser organized by Dawn awhile ago.

Suddenly the lights went out. "Hey!" Vanessa yelled.

"Boo-ah-ha-ha-ha-HA-HA-HA-HAAAAA-AAAH!" boomed a deep voice.

EEEEEEEEE, squeaked a loud door.

Step . . . CLANK. Step . . . CLANK. Step . . . CLANK. A goblin dragged its chains down the stairs.

The kids were going wild at the noises. Nicky was screaming for help (kidding, although he *did* sound scared).

Then the noises stopped and the lights went back on.

Jake and Buddy were standing by the light switch, grinning. Jake had his finger on the button of a tape recorder. "Like the tape?" Buddy asked. "It's called 'Sounds for All Occasions.' I got it out of the library."

"Would you mind keeping the lights on?" Haley asked, while signing something to her brother. Matt looked a little confused, but broke into a smile at the explanation.

His hands were now in a plateful of pinkish-white elbow macaroni. Next to the plate was an open, red plastic bottle. "Uh, may I ask what that is?" Stacey said.

"Monkey guts," Haley answered matter-of-factly. "But he has to put more red food coloring in them."

"Should he cook them first?" Mallory asked. "Then they'll feel slimier."

As Haley signed the suggestion, Nicky Pike's head called out, "Look, guys!"

Yes, his *head*. It was hanging on a wall and dripping blood. Well, actually, the wall was a white sheet on a clothesline. Nicky had cut a hole in it and stuck his head through. The blood was dark red marker.

"That is disgusting," Mallory remarked.

Stacey gasped. "Where's the rest of him?"

"Running around with no head!" Jake replied.

"He looks better that way," Vanessa said, cracking up.

Nicky stuck his tongue out at his sister. "Gee, I'm jealous, Vanessa. *You're* only missing your brains!"

"Ha-ha!" Vanessa snapped. Stacey could tell she was furiously trying to think of an insulting reply.

"Watch," Nicky said. He closed his eyes and let his head loll to the side.

Stacey had to admit he looked horrifying.

Buddy cried out, "Nicky, that looks so cool!"

"*Brrrrrup*," burped Nicky. "Excuse me."

Jake and Buddy shrieked with laughter.

"That's *really* disgusting," Mallory remarked.

"Do that in the haunted house!" Buddy urged.

"No," Vanessa said, shaking her head. "That's silly, not scary!"

"So?" Buddy said.

"This isn't a *comedy* house," Haley replied.

"So I'm just going to stand here with my eyes closed?" Nicky said. "Like, 'Duh, I'm dead'? No way!"

"Are you worried people will think you're *really* dead?" Haley asked.

"He's worried they'll *cheer*," Vanessa replied.

"Vanessa, you have no sense of humor," Nicky said, slipping his head out of the sheet.

"Oh, right. I just think burping is so funny," Vanessa retorted. "I can't stop laughing."

"You want to see something funny?" Buddy asked. He went into a corner and grabbed a rubber axe. Holding it in one hand, he began doing a jerky, Frankenstein walk toward Nicky. Slowly he raised his axe, growling.

Nicky cowered. "Hey!"

With the backswing of the axe, Buddy bopped *himself* in the forehead.

"Roooo-hoo-hoo!" he cried in a monster voice.

"That's dumb," Vanessa said.

"It is not! It's *funny*," Buddy insisted. "Little kids will love it."

Haley let out a sudden laugh. "Matt has a great idea. He can go over to a plate of guts and start eating them."

The only person laughing at that suggestion was Matt.

"Make me puke," Nicky said.

"It's just spaghetti and food coloring," Vanessa replied.

"I say no," Jake announced.

"Why?" Haley pleaded.

"Because it's going to be at my house, and

I don't want kids barfing all over the basement," Jake answered.

"You guys are being so wimpy," Haley said.

Buddy sneered at her. "Am not!"

"Are too," Vanessa chimed in.

"Am not!"

"Whoa! *Whoa!*" Mallory interrupted.

Jake, Buddy, and Nicky were standing shoulder-to-shoulder, glaring at Vanessa, Haley, and Matt. They looked like opposite sides on a battlefield.

"Um, I think you have a problem here," Stacey said calmly. "Half of you want a funny haunted house — "

"Not *just* funny," Buddy said. "*Scary* and funny."

"Okay," Stacey said. "And the other half wants just a scary haunted house."

"Scary and gross," Vanessa clarified. "That's the *definition* of a haunted house!"

"No, that's the definition of *you!*" Nicky said.

"Who's that boy who looks so icky? Oh my gosh, it must be Nicky!" Vanessa, the budding poet, taunted.

Stacey cut in before Vanessa could think of another rhyme. "How can you solve this problem?"

"We can do the haunted house by ourselves!" Nicky replied. "Just the three of us."

Buddy and Jake nodded defiantly.

"Good!" Vanessa shot back. "And we can do *our* haunted house. We don't need you."

The two sides glowered at each other. Neither was going to give an inch.

Stacey and Mal? They were relieved, in a way. At least the Funnies and the Grosses could work among themselves. The arguing would stop.

Or so they thought.

With a huge grin, Buddy said, "You'll be sorry. All the kids will be at *our* house."

"Yeah," Jake agreed, "good luck scaring each other."

"Good luck *boring* each other," Haley said.

"Hope you have buckets and barf bags for your customers," Nicky suggested.

"Hope you have sleeping bags for yours," Vanessa said.

"At least we'll *have* customers!" Jake insisted.

"We'll have *more*!" Haley retorted. "And better costumes, too!"

Stacey closed her eyes. Scare Wars had begun.

CHAPTER 10

What was I doing the weekend of Scare Wars? Not much.

I couldn't call Mrs. Kuhn.

I tried and tried, but my fingers would not finish tapping the number.

I started writing her a letter. Twice. Here's how far I got:

Dear Mrs. Kuhn,
    Please accept my apology. I certainly should not have had my boyfriend over to your house these four times without asking....

Dear Mrs. Kuhn,
    I'm so sorry about

Friday. You were right to be angry. I have always noticed that as a mother, you are doing a very good job....

Yuck. Nothing sounded right. I couldn't lie. But I couldn't tell the truth.

So I did neither. I threw away the letters.

Logan and I talked on Friday evening. Mainly he was worried about Jake's soccer game on Saturday.

"Did you tell Jake you *might* show up or *would definitely* show up?" I asked.

"Might," Logan insisted.

"I guess you shouldn't go, then, huh?" I said.

"Not without a suit of armor," Logan replied with a laugh. "Mrs. Kuhn'll be there."

Well, *not* going was a big mistake.

Saturday evening I saw Buddy coming home from the game. He said Jake looked for Logan the whole first half. Then Jake refused to play the second half and sulked on the sidelines.

I felt awful about that. So I called Logan and told him. You know what his reaction was? "That's terrible. You should have let me go."

Huh?

86

"But Logan," I pleaded, "we *both* decided it wouldn't be a good idea."

"Yeah. I guess."

The conversation didn't last much longer. I could tell Logan was angry.

Whenever someone is angry at me, the first thing I think is: *What can I do to make it better?* I just assume it's all my fault. But not this time. I mean, *Logan* was the one who ran out after the sitting job. And he never called Jake, either. He shouldn't have been angry at me.

But I didn't tell him that. In fact, I didn't tell him much of anything.

Our phone bill for the weekend was probably a record low.

I awoke Monday morning in the middle of a nightmare. In it, all my baby-sitting charges lived next door to one another. I was running desperately from house to house, ringing the bells. But each time the door opened, Mrs. Kuhn would be standing there screaming at me, calling me a liar. Finally, at the last house, she opened the door with an axe!

It was Jake's rubber axe.

Rubber or metal, it didn't matter. I was creeped out. I could barely eat breakfast. Dad and Sharon must have thought I was a zombie.

I had a terrible day at school. My friends hardly talked to me. At our BSC meeting that evening, I was left out of all the conversations.

The nicest thing anyone said to me was, "Have a Chunky."

During the whole meeting, we had only one call — Mrs. Hobart, for an early November booking. That was not a good sign.

My Tuesday was no better, except that I didn't have to put up with another BSC meeting. I called Dawn that night, but she had gone out with her family.

How were things with Logan? Well, here was what we said to each other at my locker on Wednesday morning, as far as I can remember:

Me: "Hi."

Logan: "Hi."

Me: "Practice today?"

He: "Yeah. Sure. Well. See you."

Me: " 'Bye."

In The Great Conversations of the World, it must have been last place.

I was really getting tired of this. I'd been avoiding the subject of the Kuhn Incident for three days. I decided I'd bring it up at lunch.

"Are you guys still mad at me?" I asked.

Kristy bit into a tuna sandwich. Stacey took a swig from a small bottle of mineral water. Claudia hiccuped and excused herself.

"No," Kristy said, in a way that meant *yes*.

"Not *mad*," Stacey said. "I'm just a little

concerned about . . . you know, ramifications."

I looked at Claudia.

She shrugged. "I'm not so good with my ramification tables."

We laughed politely. We ate. Alan Gray walked by with some friends and said to Kristy, "Any fingernails in your salad today?"

"Any brains in your head?" was Kristy's answer.

They exchanged a few more affectionate words, and the boys left.

That was the last we talked about my problem, until the Wednesday meeting.

I could tell things weren't going to go well, right from the start.

"Any new business?" Kristy asked.

Shannon laughed through her nose. "That's the problem. There isn't any."

Shannon hadn't meant that to sound snobby (I don't think). It was just true.

"Well, don't worry," Stacey said. "Halloween's always a busy time."

Her words kind of hung in the air, like a bad smell.

Everyone knew what the BSC record book said for October 31.

Nothing.

Not one parent had called to ask for help with trick-or-treating, or parties. Halloween was only a week and a half away.

Was it because of Mrs. Kuhn? Had she called all the parents in Stoneybrook? Had they all torn up the BSC phone number?

Rrrrrrring!

The phone. I almost jumped off the bed and did a cartwheel.

"Hello, Baby-sitters Club!" Claudia sang into the receiver. "Yes, this is she. . . ." Her smile slowly faded. "*What?* No way! I mean, no, thanks. Sorry. 'Bye."

"Who was that?" Kristy asked after Claudia hung up.

"Jasper's Legume-of-the-Month Club," Claudia replied, ashen-faced. "A different crate of beans each month, sent fresh from the farm."

"Ewwww," said Mallory.

In my mind, I took back that cartwheel.

Finally the phone did ring with a job. Mrs. Wilder needed a sitter for an hour on Thursday.

I checked the record book. "Well, I'm free, and so are Shannon and Kristy and — "

"I'll take it!" Kristy blurted out.

"Okay," I said as I marked her name in the book.

A few minutes later Mr. Ohdner called, requesting a sitter for a week from Tuesday.

"Um . . . I could do it," I said, "or Claudia or Stacey — "

"Sure!" Stacey volunteered. "Put me down."

I did.

And I put Claudia down for the next call, which was from the Prezziosos.

I was free for that one, too. And I live near the Prezziosos.

Are you getting the message? I sure was. Everyone was jumping in before I could. No one trusted me to take a job. But at least we were getting job calls again.

I had become the great embarrassment of the Baby-sitters Club.

As Claudia called back the Prezziosos to confirm, my eyes started to water. I was humiliated.

But I would not — *not* — allow myself to cry. You have no idea how hard that is for me. But I did it.

After those three calls, the phone fell silent. Claudia found some pretzels. We munched away. A little conversation started.

At 5:55, Shannon was talking about some neighbors of hers (and clients of ours), the Papadakis family. Some relatives from Greece had been visiting, and they'd stayed two weeks longer than planned.

"You should have seen Mrs. Papadakis,"

Shannon said. "She was going crazy. The relatives wanted to be taken places all the time. Only they'd never get the names right. They'd mix up American letters, like *h* and *n*. One niece insisted on going to Radio Snack."

Claudia burst into giggles at that. "Yumm!"

"Anyway, they left, and Mrs. Papadakis said she'd be calling us for lots of jobs," Shannon continued. "She and Mr. Papadakis are dying for a few nights out."

"Great!" Kristy said. "When did she tell you that?"

"Um . . . Friday."

Nobody said a word. But we were all thinking the same thing.

The Papadakises have always been steady, loyal clients. If Mrs. Kuhn called them, and convinced them to drop us, we'd be in big trouble.

At six o'clock, Kristy adjourned the meeting and quickly took off.

Stacey gave me a tiny smile as I got up. "Don't worry," she said.

I couldn't manage an answer.

I had to speak to Dawn. That was the only thought on my mind when I got home.

But at 6:15 in Connecticut, it was 3:15 in California. Dawn wouldn't be home from school yet. I called anyway, got her family's phone machine, and left a message.

An excruciating half hour later, the phone rang.

"I'll get it!" I shouted.

I ran into my parents' bedroom and picked up the receiver. "Hello?"

"Your message sounded awful, Mary Anne. Are you all right?"

Leave it to Dawn.

I couldn't hold it in. I cried and cried. In between gulps, I explained everything that had happened.

"Mary Anne," Dawn finally said. "Everything will be fine. What you did was not so horrible."

"But I *lied*!" I insisted. "And telling the truth would be *worse*, and — "

"I know how you feel. It must be so embarrassing. But it'll blow over."

"Things this serious don't just go away! Hardly anybody's calling the Baby-sitters Club anymore!"

I thought I could hear Dawn chuckle. "Look. The BSC will survive this. Parents know baby-sitters aren't perfect. Just give it some time. Soon no one will even remember this."

"You think so?"

"Yeah."

"Okay."

We chatted a little more. When we hung up, I felt a little better.

But just a little.

I decided I'd just have to live through it. I hoped Dawn was right.

Maybe I'd get the chance to baby-sit again before the age of twenty.

CHAPTER 11

D*ing-dong.*

It was Friday, around four-fifteen. When the doorbell rang, I was in the middle of a very long math homework problem.

No, I did not have homework on a Friday. I was just studying for a test the next week. Why? I had nothing else to do. All of my friends were baby-sitting. Often *I* am, too, at that hour.

But that was before I became the official BSCO — Baby-sitters Club Outcast.

"Tiggy, can you get that?" I asked.

Tigger gave me a look and rubbed his back against my ankle.

Ding-dong.

Sharon and Dad were at work. I had to answer it.

With a sigh, I put down my pencil and went downstairs. I hoped it wasn't a salesperson. I always want to say yes because I feel so sorry for them.

Before I got to the door, I took a peek through the living room windows.

It was not a salesperson.

It was Mrs. Kuhn and Jake.

Did she see me? I wasn't sure. I thought of running out the back door. Or sinking to the floor and hiding.

Why was she here? To yell at me again? To tell me how hurt Jake was? To make a citizen's arrest?

Knock-knock-knock.

I was being ridiculous. Nothing bad would happen. I told myself not to be scared. I stood up straight and grabbed the doorknob.

Besides, I could see someone raking Mrs. Prezzioso's lawn. If Mrs. Kuhn tried to hit me, I'd have a witness.

I pulled the door open calmly, smiled, and said, "Hulllk."

Charming. It was supposed to be "Hello," but my throat was dry as paper.

I swallowed and tried again. "Hi, Jake. Hi, Mrs. Kuhn."

"Hello, Mary Anne. May we come in?" asked Mrs. Kuhn.

"Sure," I replied, backing inside.

We stood in the middle of the living room. Jake was looking around uncomfortably. I sud-

96

denly remembered my manners.

"Have a seat," I said, gesturing to the sofa. "Would you like something to eat or drink?"

Jake's eyes lit up. "Yea — "

"Not right now, thank you," Mrs. Kuhn replied, sitting down. "I don't want to stay long. I have something to say to you. I thought of calling, but I decided I'd rather see you face-to-face."

Gulp.

I sat in an armchair. I had to. My knees buckled.

"This has been such a busy week for me," she began. "I should have talked to Jake about this sooner, but so it goes. At any rate, we spoke today about your boyfriend."

"Yes?" I said softly.

"Well, Jake just hasn't been the same since last Friday."

"He was supposed to come to my soccer game," Jake informed me.

"I had no idea Logan was coaching Jake in soccer," Mrs. Kuhn went on. "I had thought . . . well, I had been confused. At any rate, Jake told me that Logan was spending all his time with *him*, while you looked after the girls."

"Yes." I felt my head slowly sinking.

"That he went straight to the backyard,

played sports with Jake, and left soon afterward."

"Uh-huh."

Mrs. Kuhn took a deep breath. "Well, to tell you the truth, Mary Anne, I think that's . . ."

She seemed to be searching for a word. I glanced up at her and noticed her eyes seemed a little misty. I *knew* it. She'd been insulted. Hurt.

"Wonderful," was her next word.

At least that was what it sounded like.

"Excuse me?" I said.

"I'm afraid I owe you an apology, Mary Anne. I don't know how I could have been so harsh. Jake told me how much Logan's visits meant to him. Logan was like a real big brother." She smiled and ran her fingers gently through her son's hair. "And goodness knows, Jake could use a male presence around the house."

I almost fainted. *Male presence?* Those were the exact words I'd been too afraid to say in front of her.

"Logan is the *best* athlete!" Jake piped up.

"Yeah, he really is," I agreed.

Then I looked at Mrs. Kuhn. Her eyes were kind and smiling, the way they'd always been before last week. "Of course I accept your apology," I said.

"I'm puzzled about one thing, Mary Anne.

Why didn't you tell me this on Friday?"

I sighed. "I guess I was afraid you'd get the wrong message. That I was *meddling* or something. Trying to do your job. Trying to make up for . . . you know. . . ."

I didn't want to come right out and talk about Jake's dad. Not while Jake was there.

But I could tell Mrs. Kuhn knew exactly what I meant. "On the contrary," she said. "That was about the most compassionate thing you could have done."

Oh, boy. Tears were filling my eyes. I thought they'd back up into my head and come out my ears. "I . . . I guess I should apologize, too," I said. "If I'd told the truth, Jake wouldn't have had such a bad week."

"Aw, that's all right," Jake replied, bouncing on the sofa. "I can play with him again, right?"

"Right!" Mrs. Kuhn and I said together.

"Cool," was his response.

Mrs. Kuhn stood up with a broad smile. "I'd like to tell Logan what I told you, and personally invite him to the house. So if you give me his number, I'll call this afternoon — "

"Call from here!" Jake blurted out.

He and I looked hopefully at Mrs. Kuhn. She shrugged. "Why not?"

Jake thrust his fist into the air and cried out, "*Yyyyes!*"

I wrote down Logan's number and Mrs. Kuhn took it to the kitchen phone.

Jake and I hung out in the living room and heard snatches of conversation. Just as she was about to hang up, Jake called out, "Can he come over?"

"Excuse me," Mrs. Kuhn said into the phone. She covered the receiver and asked Jake, "You mean, now?"

"Yeah!" Jake replied.

Logan must have heard through her palm, because Mrs. Kuhn smiled and said, "It's all right with him."

"It's all right with me, too," I added.

"And me!" Jake agreed.

"Come on over," Mrs. Kuhn said to Logan.

"Double *yyyyes!*" Jake cheered.

Well, guess who got an instant sitting job? Mrs. Kuhn needed to pick up her daughters from an after-school program, so she had to leave Jake at my house — and she insisted on paying her regular rate.

It felt great to be wanted again.

You know what else? Mrs. Kuhn promised to call Kristy before the meeting and explain everything. That was a big relief.

At about ten to five, the doorbell rang.

"I'll get it!" Jake shouted, running to the door.

I don't know who was happier to see Logan's smile, Jake or me.

Logan had a soccer ball in his right hand. "Last one to the barn door is a plate of sweetbreads."

Jake ran outside in a shot. He screamed with laughter as he raced Logan to the barn.

For the next twenty minutes, they played like crazy. Then we walked Jake home. And guess what? Mrs. Kuhn invited Logan and me for dinner after the BSC meeting.

A job, a boyfriend, a dinner date — all in one afternoon!

I held Logan's hand on the way to the meeting. The colors on the trees were stunning. We both smiled the whole way.

CHAPTER 12

"Uh-huh . . . oh . . . yeah . . . uh-huh . . . mmm . . ."

That was Kristy's side of a phone conversation as Logan and I walked into BSC headquarters.

We were the last to arrive. Logan hardly ever attends meetings, so the other members looked a little puzzled.

"Right. . . . Yeah, she just got here, with Logan."

I knew Kristy was talking to Mrs. Kuhn. And I could tell Claudia, Stacey, Shannon, Mallory, and Jessi had no clue what was going on.

"I'm starving," was Logan's greeting. "Got any chocolate, Claudia?"

Of course, that's like asking a fish in a pond if it has any water. Claudia brought out an assortment: Milk Duds, Heath Bars, and M&M's.

By the time Kristy got off the phone, everyone in the room (except Stacey) was munching away.

"This meeting will come to order!" Kristy bellowed.

Munch, munch, munch, we replied.

"You guys look like goats," Kristy said.

"Baaaaah," Claudia replied.

"Well, I have decided not to disband the Baby-sitters Club after all," Kristy announced.

A big "Huh?" went up from us all.

"Just joking." Kristy smiled. "That was Mrs. Kuhn. Remember how scared we were? Well, she never told one parent what happened with Logan and Mary Anne. In fact, she thinks Mary Anne is great and the BSC is fantastic."

"I could have told her that," Logan said.

"Mm-hm," Kristy replied with a raised eyebrow. "You could have told her a few things at the beginning, and none of this would have happened."

Logan sank downward, slowly hiding behind me. Then he began whimpering like a dog.

"Excuse me, *what* is going on?" Stacey asked. "How did she change her mind?"

Kristy explained everything — how Jake had told Mrs. Kuhn about Logan, how they both had talked to me, how much Logan meant to Jake.

The other girls stopped chewing. As they listened, their faces began to change a little, to loosen up. For the first time in a while, I began *not* feeling like an intruder at someone else's party.

"Anyway," Kristy continued, "Mrs. Kuhn says that Jake never used to be terribly interested in sports. Today, when she asked him to help make a salad, he brought the ball into the kitchen with him."

"It's a little big for a crouton," Claudia remarked. "But if he sliced it in half, it would make a great bowl."

Kristy ignored the joke. "She practically had to wrestle the ball away from him. He quickly cut up carrots or whatever, and now he's back outside, kicking the ball around like a pro, or so she says. Anyway, I could hear him. He was yelling the same thing over and over at the top of his lungs — "

"Don't tell me," Logan cut in. " '*Yyyyy-yess!*' "

"Yes!" Kristy repeated.

"Wow," Mallory said. "That doesn't sound like the Jake I know."

Claudia smiled at me. "So you didn't mess up after all, Mary Anne."

I shrugged. The rain gutters above my eyes were starting to fill again.

Shannon looked sheepish. "And we were

giving you such a hard time."

"That was dumb of us," Jessi commented.

Stacey nodded. "We were so worried about the *club*. Like the whole world was going to fall apart because of what Mary Anne did."

"Having a club doesn't mean anything if we don't support each other," Jessi remarked.

"Yeah." Kristy took off her visor. She scratched her head. She cleared her throat and glanced out the window. "Sorry."

That's about as emotional as Kristy gets. But somehow, her apology meant the most.

"All in favor of saying I'm sorry to Mary Anne, say 'Aye,' " Claudia said in an official-sounding voice.

"Aye!" everyone shouted.

That was when the gutter overflowed. I buried my head in Logan's shirt and cried and cried and cried. If my cheeks were made of soil, I'd have raised a garden.

Logan sighed. "This shirt needed to be washed, anyway."

"All in favor of saying I'm sorry to *Logan*, say, 'Awww,' " Claudia announced.

"Awwww . . ."

Everyone cracked up. Me included.

Well, everyone except Logan. He was blushing.

Rrrrrrring!

Claudia snatched up the receiver. "New, improved Baby-sitters Club! Oh, hi, Mrs. Papadakis. . . . Wait. Monday afternoon, Wednesday night, *and* trick-or-treating on Halloween? Okay, I'll call you back."

The moment she hung up, Kristy leaped off her director's seat. "Yah-*hoooooo*! A triple play!"

"Ahem. A little dignity, please?" Claudia said. "Ms. Secretary?"

I quickly opened the book. "Well, I can do Monday, and so can Mallory and Shannon. . . ."

"It's yours," Mal said, and Shannon nodded in agreement.

I couldn't help grinning. "Let's see, on Wednesday — "

Rrrrrrring!

"Hello? Hi, Dr. Johanssen! Charlotte needs help making her costume? On Thursday? Just a minute."

"Stacey, you're free," I whispered.

"Okay," Stacey said to Claudia.

(Stacey and Charlotte are super-close, so Stace usually gets first chance at the Johanssen house.)

"You're all set, Dr. Johanssen," Claudia said. "You're welcome. 'Bye." *Click.*

Rrrrrrring!

Kristy was wide-eyed. "I don't believe this!"

It was Mr. Newton, needing help for Jamie's Halloween party. Mallory took that one.

Rrrrrrring!

Mrs. Marshall, wanting someone to take Nina and Eleanor trick-or-treating. That was Claudia's.

Our heads were spinning by 5:59. Kristy was giving high-fives all around. Claudia put on a CD and started dancing. I closed the record book and Logan gave me a big hug.

With one eye on the clock, Kristy declared, "This meeting is now adjour — "

"Wait!" I called out. "The Papadakises!"

Claudia turned off the CD player. "Yikes! We have to call her back!"

I began leafing through the record book again. Six o'clock and we *still* had not finished assigning jobs. What a change.

It felt absolutely fantastic.

CHAPTER 13

"And soooo . . ." Laurel Kuhn recited in a spooky voice, "the wicked witch picked up her broom and cackled, 'Eeeeee-heh-heh-heh!' "

"Not so loud!" Patsy begged her.

The den was dark, except for the light peeking in under the door. It was Tuesday, three days before Halloween. The Kuhn sisters were telling me a story they had made up, complete with sound effects and special lighting (well, flashlights held under their faces).

Boy, was I happy to be sitting for the Kuhns again. You know what? Mrs. Kuhn had requested me specifically — and had asked if I could bring Logan along!

Logan said he wanted to come, so Jake was eagerly waiting in the kitchen. He had not been interested in hearing the girls' story, "The Girl and the Horrible Witch."

"But as the witch tried to fly away . . . 'Oh,

no!' she said. 'It's not flying.' " Laurel paused dramatically.

"And the little girl who she scared?" Patsy continued. "You know, the one with the red hair? Well, this time *she* snuck up on the witch . . . slowly . . . slowly . . . slo-o-owly, and. . . ."

"BOOOOOO!" The den door flew open, sending in a flood of light.

"Aaaaaaaugh!" The girls shrieked.

Jake stood in the doorway, snickering. "Gotcha!"

Patsy was crying. "You *scared* me!"

Laurel stood up, her fists clenched. "I hate you, you fat old ugly — "

She lunged toward him. Jake ran through the house, giggling.

Ding-dong!

Jake scooted into the living room and yanked the door open. "Logan!" he said.

"Yooooooooou!" Laurel stormed into the room behind Jake, then stopped in her tracks.

That was when I walked in. There was Logan, smiling down at Jake and his sister. Laurel stood there, fists in the air, ready to burst but too embarrassed.

"Laurel's practicing her alphabet," Jake teased. "That was a very good *U*, Laurel. Now try *veeeeeeeee.*"

"Jake!" I warned.

Laurel folded her arms and stomped away. "Go kick your stupid ball around!"

Logan looked at me and rolled his eyes. "Come on, Jake-o," he said. "Let's talk."

I went back into the den with the girls. They put a chair against the door.

"And so . . ." Patsy said, "the little girl grabbed the broom and said, 'The magic spell is gone!' And the witch slowly shriveled away."

"But as she did," Laurel continued, "the girl felt something strange in her mouth. Her teeth seemed to be growing. And her hair felt kind of dry. So she took the broom and turned to go inside. But as she opened her mouth to call her mom, she said, 'Eeeeee-heh-heh-heh!' "

"And she flew away!" Patsy said. "The end!"

"Yeaaaa!" I cheered.

Laurel flicked on the light. "Now can you help us make our costumes? Mom helped us pick fabric and stuff, but we have to put it together."

"Sure," I said.

We left the den. Patsy and Laurel ran upstairs to get the material.

Logan and Jake were sitting at the kitchen table. Jake was explaining about the two haunted houses. "So Vanessa and Haley and

Matt said they wanted their own! They are such babies." Jake shook his head. "Now they're dead meat. Ours is going to be so much better."

"What's *in* this haunted house?" Logan asked.

"Want to see?"

"You bet!"

Jake bolted out of his chair. "Come on. Maybe you can *help* us!"

"Well, sure," Logan said. "I guess — "

"You can?" Jake let out a howl of triumph. "*Yyyyess!* Wait, I have to call Buddy and Nicky!"

He went to the phone and began tapping out a number.

Logan and I exchanged a smile. "Kids," he said with a shrug.

"Hi, can I speak to Buddy?" Jake said into the receiver. "You will not believe this! Logan's going to make our haunted house with us!" I could hear Buddy cheering through the phone and across the kitchen.

"Are you sure you want to do this?" I asked Logan.

"Yeah!" Logan said. "Hey, we'll *cream* them."

"Logan, you're worse than they are."

"What do you mean?"

"Well, you're so much *older*. Isn't it kind of

unfair if you help? Jake's house is going to have such an advantage."

Logan laughed. "It's not a big deal, Mary Anne. Besides, how do you know no one's helping Vanessa?"

Before I could answer, the girls ran downstairs with a cardboard box and a sewing basket. "Come on!" Patsy called to me.

We headed back into the den. I opened the box and pulled out a black, pointed hat. Under it was a long piece of black material and a white sheet.

"I'm a witch and Patsy's a ghost," Laurel announced.

"Okay, witch," I said. "Get up on a chair and I'll fit you."

I tried to make it simple. I draped the material around her in a loose, flowing style.

Then Buddy's face appeared in the den window. "I see London, I see France, I see Laurel's underpants!" he sang.

"You do not!" Laurel screamed.

"Get out of here!" Patsy shouted.

Laughing, Buddy ran around back.

Before long Nicky arrived. The boys all went into the basement with Logan. I'm not sure exactly what they did down there. I heard scraping sounds, hammering, talking, and giggling.

"What are they *doing*?" Laurel asked.

Just then Patsy cried out, "Hey! What happened to Herman? He was on the windowsill."

The girls' skeleton was missing.

"*Jake!*" Patsy screamed, running out of the room.

I have to admit that even though I was happy to be sitting again, I was not looking forward to Friday.

CHAPTER 14

FRIDAY - HALLOWEEN !!
I was supposed to spend an hour with Marilyn and Carolyn Arnold. They were supposed to be ready to go when I got there. I was supposed to be home in time to take my sisters trick-or-treating.
How did everything get so complicated?

*B*oiiiing.
Boiiiing.
Boiiiing.

When Shannon got to the Arnolds' house, Marilyn and Carolyn were bouncing off each other.

Yes, bouncing. They had on matching striped pajamas, stuffed with pillows in the front and back.

Mrs. Arnold had called Claudia's that day, saying she'd lost a contact lens and had to go to the eye doctor for an emergency replacement. Claudia had just gotten home from school. She quickly looked at the record book, then called Shannon, who was the only one not working on Halloween.

Shannon had a *little* time, because her youngest sister was at after-school swimming. So she took the job.

And that's how she ended up with the bouncing twins.

As their bellies collided, Marilyn and Carolyn giggled hysterically.

"Hello?" Shannon called through the screen door.

"Hi!" the twins squealed.

Mrs. Arnold came running into the living room. She was wearing an old pair of granny glasses. "Oh, thank you for coming at such short notice. I didn't get a chance to finish getting the girls ready, but you can do that. There's makeup in the bathroom. I gave the girls money to go to that haunted house. I'll be back from the eye doctor in an hour, and then I'll drive you home, okay? 'Bye!"

Zoom. Off she went.

"Uh, let me guess," Shannon said. "Tigers?"

"No," the twins answered.

"Bees?"

"Nooo."

"I give up."

"I'm Tweedledee and she's Tweedledum," Carolyn said.

"Wait, you're Tweedledum," Marilyn replied.

"I'm *dee*, not *dum!*"

"I'm not going to be *dum!*"

"It's just a name, Marilyn!"

"Uh, girls, I think we better get going," Shannon said gently.

"But we have to do makeup!" Carolyn protested. "Mom put some in the bathroom."

"Let's go," Shannon said. "We don't have to tell anyone which Tweedle is which."

They ran into the bathroom, where Mrs. Arnold had left out some rouge and eyeliner,

116

plus a brand-new pack of different colored wax sticks.

Shannon went wild. She drew handlebar mustaches on them both. She gave them rosy cheeks. She blackened out teeth. She slicked their hair back and sprayed it.

When they were done, Marilyn ran into her bedroom. She emerged with a huge plastic rattle shaped like a pretzel.

"Tweedledum and Tweedledee agreed to go to battle," she recited. "Cause Tweedledee, said Tweedledum, had broke his brand-new rattle!"

"Boinng!" cried Carolyn, bouncing into her sister.

The twins ran to the living room. On the table was a pair of ski caps and two folded plastic shopping bags. They put the hats on, grabbed the bags, and ran outside.

Shannon rushed after them. She could not stop giggling. The twins' pillows kept lumping up in different places. They kept having to yank them up.

At house after house, neighbors burst out laughing. Unfortunately most of them said, "Munchkins!"

As the twins approached the Goldmans' house, Marilyn mumbled, "If I hear Munchkins once more, I'll scream."

Mr. and Mrs. Goldman are a friendly, elderly couple who love kids. They opened the door together, smiling. "Goodness, Munchkins!" Mr. Goldman said.

"*Yeeaaaaaaaagh!*" screamed Marilyn.

(Well, she'd promised.)

The Goldmans' smiles fell. "Well, those are some hunger pains, huh?" Mrs. Goldman remarked. "Better take two."

She dropped two enormous Milky Way bars in each girl's bag. The girls yelped "Thanks!" and skipped away.

"Hey, that worked great," Carolyn said. "I think I'll try it next time."

Shannon gave her a Look. "Uh, no. I value my hearing."

Down the block, they ran into Claudia, who was taking around Nina and Eleanor Marshall. Nina's four, and she had on a green dragon costume. Eleanor, who's two, was wearing a blue leotard and a tophat.

"Hey!" Claudia greeted us. "It's Tweedledum and Tweedledee!"

"I *knew* she'd guess it!" Marilyn exclaimed.

"Don't tell me." Shannon looked carefully at the Marshall girls. "A dragon and . . . a toddler!"

"Naaaaaoooo," Eleanor said with her bashful smile. "Toss the *Tankinger!*"

"What a vocabulary," Shannon remarked. "What did she say?"

"Thomas the Tank Engine," Nina translated. "The hat is her smokestack."

They hit the next few houses together, then met up with Mallory, who was with Margo and Claire.

Margo was jumping with excitement. "You guys *have* to go to Vanessa's haunted house. It is *soooo* scary. Kids are screaming! You know Todd Masters? He *cried*."

Marilyn and Carolyn did not look too psyched. "Scary?" Marilyn said.

"Yeah," Margo replied. "It's much better than dumb old Jake's. His isn't scary. It's just *funny*. Some haunted house!"

"Have you been there, too?" Claudia asked.

"No way, José," Claire said.

With that, the Pike sisters skipped to the next house.

" 'Bye!" Mallory called, chasing after them.

Claudia whispered to the twins, "Don't worry. If you go to the funny one, I'm sure they'll still be your friends."

Carolyn and Marilyn both grinned. "Okay," Marilyn said. "Let's go to Jake's."

Shannon looked at her watch. In twelve minutes, Mrs. Arnold was supposed to pick her up. "All right, but we have to make it quick," she said.

The girls gave Shannon their bags, which were weighted down with candy. As they scampered on ahead, Shannon lugged the bags behind them.

She was out of breath when they got to the hand-made sign in front of the Kuhns' house:

HAUNTED HOUSE!!
YOU'LL SCREAM WITH FRIGHT—
IF YOU DON'T DIE LAUGHING!
ONLY 50 CENTS
(FREE IF YOU DON'T SURVIVE)

(If you detect Logan's sense of humor, you're right. He thought up the sign. And drew it.)

Mrs. Kuhn had hired me to help greet the trick-or-treaters. When I opened the door for Marilyn and Carolyn, they looked petrified.

"Hi!" I said. "Are you here for the haunted house?"

"Yes," replied Carolyn.

"No," replied Marilyn.

"Marilyn!" her sister cried. "Don't be a chicken."

"Oh, all right."

Shannon sighed. "Wish us luck," she said under her breath.

Into the kitchen they went.

"Grrrreetings! Beware all who enter!"

Marilyn and Carolyn gaped. A corpse was speaking to them from the top of the stairs. His skin was pasty white and his teeth brown-stained. His eyes were ringed with red, his lips with black. His hair was mussed and his clothes in tatters.

Logan the Undead.

"Um, maybe we should go home," Marilyn suggested.

"Hey, it's just me," Logan said in his normal voice.

"Buck-buck-buck," Carolyn clucked like a chicken.

Marilyn took a deep breath. "Okay. Let's go."

They paid their fifty cents and descended the Stairs to the Underworld. Cobwebs were strung along the walls, with fake spiders inside them. In the center of one complicated-looking web was a sign that said SOME PIG.

Marilyn smiled. "Charlotte!" she cried.

"Johanssen?" Carolyn asked.

"No, silly. Charlotte's Web!"

From below, Jake's voice boomed out (through a mike attached to a children's tape recorder): *"Welcome to the Mysterious and Deadly Underwear!"*

Carolyn lost it. She howled with laughter. "Underwear?"

"Oops. Er, I meant Underworld. Enter through the curtains if you dare!"

At the bottom of the stairs were two blankets, suspended by rope, that prevented light from entering the haunted house.

Whhhoooooo . . . eeeeeee . . .

Jake's sound effects tape was making wind noises and eerie squeaks.

Carolyn and Marilyn timidly walked through the curtains. The basement was spookily lit, with dim blue lights that Logan had bought at the hardware store.

Jake had decided against Jason and the seaweed. He stood just inside the curtain, dressed as Dracula. He wore his plastic fangs. He held out a plastic Mickey Mouse mug filled with red liquid and labelled BLOOD. (It was actually Kool-Aid.) "May I offer you a . . . Bloody Mary? Ha-ha-ha-ha!"

"Eww," Marilyn said.

"Look." Carolyn pointed to one corner, where the shadow of a skeleton danced lazily behind a thin white sheet.

Yes, it was Herman. He was moving in the breeze of a fan placed behind him.

Pushing aside more cobwebs, the twins

made their way around the basement, toward a table. On top of it were three shoeboxes. A hole had been cut in the side of each, just big enough for a small hand to reach through. One box was labelled EYES OF NEWT, another INTESTINES OF RAT, and the third GOAT BRAINS.

"Yuck!"

"Gross!"

"Ew!"

The twins had to feel each one.

Another "curtain" hung just beyond the table. Behind it, Nicky moaned, "Ohhh, I lost my head! Who did this to me?"

Carolyn and Marilyn hurried toward the sound.

"Aaaaaagh!"

They both shrieked as a headless body, dressed in black and wielding an axe, jumped out from behind the curtain.

He swung a few times wildly, while the twins caught their breath. Then he walked into a wall. "Ow."

Behind the curtain, Nicky's head was hanging on the sheet, just as he'd practiced. He rolled his eyes and shouted to the body, "Over here, dummy."

Well, by the time Shannon had to go, Tweedles Dum and Dee were ready to do battle.

They did *not* want to leave the haunted house.

"It's so early!" Marilyn protested.

"We hardly got *any* candy!" Carolyn insisted, struggling to lift her treat bag. "No fair!"

I don't know how Shannon finally managed to get them back to their house. And when she did, Mrs. Arnold hadn't arrived!

Finally Mrs. Arnold pulled up, fifteen minutes late. "Hop in, everybody!" she called out her window.

All the way to the Kilbournes' house, Mrs. Arnold apologized again and again.

Shannon sweetly said it was okay. Then she bolted out of the car and ran into her house, anxious and guilty for being late.

"She's here!" yelled Tiffany, Shannon's eleven-year-old sister. She ran into the living room with an unzipped tutu (part of a Tinker Bell costume). Holding out a string of small bells, she asked, "Can you zip me, and put these around my neck?"

Then Maria Kilbourne, who's eight, came racing into the room. "Tie this for me, please!"

She was holding out a camouflage-pattern bandanna that was part of her jungle fighter outfit.

"One at a time!" Shannon pleaded. Then she called out, "Mom?"

Mrs. Kilbourne came in from the kitchen.

"Shannon! I just left a message on the Arnolds' machine. I didn't know where you were. What happened?"

"Ow!" Tiffany cried as the zipper caught her skin.

"Isn't anybody going to help me?" demanded Maria.

Shannon managed to get her sisters ready, answer her mom, and leave the house.

She doesn't remember much about the actual trick-or-treating — except that it lasted a long time.

She *does* remember collapsing on her bed afterward, exhausted. And hearing the phone ring. And picking it up to hear Kristy saying, "Shannon, I just spoke to Mary Anne. You will not *believe* what happened with the haunted houses tonight."

CHAPTER 15

"How was it?" I asked Ben, James, Mathew, and Johnny Hobart as they emerged from the haunted house.

"Great!" Ben replied. (Actually, it sounded more like "Groit." The Hobarts are from Australia.)

"Better than the other one," Mathew remarked.

"Well, this one was *good*," James said. "But the other one had *much* scarier special effects."

"Yeah," Johnny piped up. "Yuckier, too."

Two thumbs up, two thumbs down.

I wasn't surprised that people liked Jake's house. I mean, Jake *had* had some professional help (well, Logan). To tell you the truth, I'd felt sorry for Vanessa and her gang.

But I had been polling the kids all evening, and guess what? Scare Wars was a close race. The two Hobart boys were not the only ones who liked the Braddocks' house better.

I was impressed.

It had been a fun evening for me. Let me backtrack to the beginning.

I'd arrived around four-thirty. I helped Mrs. Kuhn fill the candy bowl and put up some decorations. I also helped fill the shoeboxes with olives (for the eyes of newt), oiled rubber gloves (for rats' intestines), and Jell-O (for goat brains). Mrs. Kuhn was even more grossed out than I was.

Just before we brought the delectable boxes downstairs, I knocked on the bathroom door. "Are you done with your makeup?" I asked.

"Not so loud," Logan replied. "What if King were bringing some kids over and heard you?"

"Sorry."

He was right. Some of those teammates of his would *never* let him forget he used makeup. That's even worse than baby-sitting!

Talk about immature.

Anyway, I carried the boxes downstairs with Mrs. Kuhn. Just inside the first curtain, Buddy was struggling with an oversized black sweatshirt. "It won't stay over my head!"

"Stay right there!" Mrs. Kuhn said. She put the boxes down and went upstairs to get a sewing kit.

Minutes later she had narrowed the opening

of Buddy's collar. When he put the sweatshirt on, his head couldn't go through. "Do I look headless?"

He didn't. Mrs. Kuhn and I went to work, stuffing the saggy area above his shoulders with crumpled newspapers.

Ding-dong!

"A customer!" Nicky yelled from behind his curtain.

"Where's Logan?" Jake asked in a panic.

"Up here!" Logan shouted from upstairs. "Bring them on!"

Mrs. Kuhn and I ran upstairs. Scare Wars had begun.

Shannon and the twins were some of our first customers. They were lucky. They had the whole haunted house to themselves. But soon the word started getting around, and the basement became crazy.

Bobby Gianelli pulled the olives out of the box and ate one. That made his younger sister wail.

Norman Hill was so surprised by Buddy's axe routine that he pushed Buddy and sent him flying against Nicky's sheet. The sheet tore down and we had to close the haunted house for repairs.

When the sound effects tape ended, Jake turned it over, but he didn't read the label. So for a few seconds, the haunted house was echoing with farm animal noises.

Logan's makeup scared one little girl so badly she ran out of the house, screaming.

But all in all, I'd say it was a big success.

Around eight o'clock the trick-or-treaters began to taper off. The candy in the bowl had dwindled. I was feeling happy (and full — Mrs. Kuhn and I had been sneaking a candy bar here and there).

Logan wandered into the living room. He had sweated off most of his makeup. "Do you think the Braddocks have closed up yet?" he asked.

"I doubt it," Mrs. Kuhn said.

I was dying of curiosity. "Mrs. Kuhn, would you mind if Logan and I went to see it?"

"Not at all. We're fine here. Besides, Buddy's due to go home soon. Then we'll have to close up."

"Thanks!"

Logan ran into the bathroom and washed up. Then we said good-bye to the kids downstairs and ran over to the Braddocks' house.

The enemy camp.

A large, unfamiliar man was sitting in a chair on the Braddocks' porch. Large, unfamiliar, and ugly.

As we got closer we saw the man was actually a sweatsuit stuffed with newspapers. Its face was a pumpkin covered with a mask and wearing a baseball hat.

Mr. Braddock answered the door. "Heyyy, welcome! Here to see the competition, eh? Go on down!"

He escorted us through the house and gestured to the basement stairs.

Smoke was billowing up!

"Dry ice," Mr. Braddock said with a wink. "I have a friend who works with the stuff."

Logan and I walked downward. The mist was coming from a large barrel. Haley was behind it, stirring with a long stick. She was in her Madame Leveaux outfit, which had been modified to look witchlike.

Behind her, Vanessa lay in a coffin.

Well, it was a refrigerator box on its side. But it had been painted black on the outside and red on the inside.

"Ohhhhhhh," Vanessa moaned. Slowly, with a grim expression, she opened her eyes.

Her face broke into a smile. "Mary Anne!"

Suddenly she frowned again and tried to look dead.

Haley glared at us. "You wake zee dead from her sleep. You must suffer, suffer deep. My vat contains a dragon's breath. It will give you life — or death!"

She began stirring with the stick. "Now eet's

130

time to meet your doom. Enter zee forbidden room!"

With a flourish, she pointed to a door to our left.

"Great!" Logan began applauding, but Haley just stamped her foot and kept pointing. I nudged him. "Oops," he said. "Sorry."

The "finished" section of the Braddocks' basement is surrounded by walls of wood paneling. Behind the walls are a few small rooms, including the one Vanessa was pointing to.

We opened the door, went inside, and shut it behind us.

The room was pitch-black. Then, *click!* A dim purple light went on.

Suddenly a skeleton appeared. It seemed to be floating just above the ground. It looked around the room and then saw us. Slowly it approached, raising its arms as if to attack.

"RRRRAAAAAAAA!" it bellowed.

We watched in fascination. I'd seen "black light" used in a stage show before. It only lights up white objects, leaving everything else in darkness.

The door opened and Haley poked her head in. "Usually by now the people are screaming," she explained.

We could see the skeleton now. It was Matt, in a black costume with a white skeleton printed on it. He ripped off his mask and grinned.

I grinned back. "You were great, Matt!" I said.

Haley signed to him, and he beamed in response.

Then he led us to his prized display of monkey guts. Boy, did they look revolting — spaghetti, elbow macaroni, ziti noodles, and unidentified thick glops, all colored brick red.

"I think I'm going to get sick," Logan said.

Just then Vanessa began moaning again. This time she got up from her coffin and began shuffling toward us. She was dressed in rags, her face was chalk white, and she was missing one hand. She had it tucked inside her sleeve (I hoped), which was painted dark red.

"My . . . hand!" she screamed. "My . . . hand!"

She lunged toward us, but we got out of the way.

When we turned around, she was staring at the floor, at a grave made with a cardboard tombstone and lots of plastic Easter-basket grass.

Sticking out of the grass was a hand. A rubber, motorized hand that wiggled and writhed, as if it wanted to break out of the ground.

"Ugh!" I said. But I wasn't grossed out. Not

really. I'd seen that hand before — or one just like it.

"Wow," Logan whispered to me. "This is an amazing haunted house."

"Mm-hm," I replied.

"You were worried about unfairness? These guys did *great* without any help."

"I guess," I said.

"You underestimate the kids." Logan wandered over to a card table. A sheet was draped over the top, reaching all the way to the floor. On the sheet was a hat box with a hole in the top. It looked something like Jake's shoeboxes, only it had the words DANGER: DO NOT TOUCH CREATURE INSIDE on it.

Of course Logan reached inside it.

"Yyyeeaaaaaaaagh!"

I have never heard Logan scream like that. He tried to pull his hand away, but it wasn't coming out.

With a sudden, strong jerk, he yanked his hand free.

The table tipped. The box slid off, taking the sheet with it.

Then, with a crash, the table fell to the floor.

The first thing I noticed was that the table had a hole in it.

The second thing I noticed was the guy sitting where the table had been.

Alan Gray. Owner of the Disgusto Hand.

Grinning his Official Pest-of-the-Eighth-Grade smile.

"I don't believe this," I said, shaking my head.

"What are you doing here?" Logan asked.

Alan sneered. "Hey, I like helping children."

"I told Mallory we wanted our haunted house to be gross and disgusting," Vanessa explained. "And she said, 'Call Alan Gray, he's an expert.' "

Alan was turning red. Behind him, the mechanical hand was making a whirring noise.

Logan put his hand over his mouth, but it was too late. He exploded with laughter.

I couldn't help it. I did, too.

I couldn't wait to tell Kristy.

About the Author

ANN M. MARTIN did *a lot* of baby-sitting when she was growing up in Princeton, New Jersey. She is a former editor of books for children, and was graduated from Smith College.

Ms. Martin lives in New York City with her cats, Mouse and Rosie. She likes ice cream and *I Love Lucy*; and she hates to cook.

Ann Martin's Apple Paperbacks include *Yours Turly, Shirley*; *Ten Kids, No Pets*; *With You and Without You*; *Bummer Summer*; and all the other books in the Baby-sitters Club series.

Look for #80

MALLORY PIKE, #1 FAN

I stared at the name happily. How unbelievably great!

My eyes traveled over to the address — and I nearly fell to the floor. Henrietta Hayes lived on Morgan Road, in Stoneybrook! Morgan Road is off Burnt Hill Road. Dawn's and Mary Anne's house is on Burnt Hill Road. Logan lives on Burnt Hill, too.

All this time Logan, Dawn, and Mary Anne had been Henrietta Hayes's neighbors and they didn't even know it!

The important thing was that I'd found her. With the phone book in my arms, I went back upstairs to my room. By flashlight, I wrote Henrietta Hayes a third letter.

Dear Ms. Hayes, I've just finished reading Alice Anderson's Big Break. It is the funniest book I've ever read. I'm sad that there is only one more Alice book left for me to read.

I really hope you are working on more. Since I've discovered your work, I've become your number one fan. You may already know all this because I've written you before. My problem is that this time, I need you to write me back a real letter. It's important because my class project, which counts for almost my whole grade for this marking period, depends on it.

I went on to tell her about the project. I told her every detail, about how Mr. Williams hadn't liked it until I added the part about comparing and contrasting my experience as an author with her own. (I wanted her to know she was a big part of this.) I mentioned that we were neighbors and that I had friends who lived close to her on Burnt Hill Road. (I thought that might appeal to her sense of neighborliness.) By the time the letter was finished, it was three pages long. For a finishing touch, I wrote out an envelope with my name and address on it. *P.S.*, I added to the bottom of my letter. *This self-addressed stamped envelope is enclosed for your convenience. I hope you can write back soon since time is running out.*

by Ann M. Martin

More titles... ▶

The Baby-sitters Club titles continued...

❑ MG45659-8	#58 Stacey's Choice	$3.50
❑ MG45660-1	#59 Mallory Hates Boys (and Gym)	$3.50
❑ MG45662-8	#60 Mary Anne's Makeover	$3.50
❑ MG45663-6	#61 Jessi's and the Awful Secret	$3.50
❑ MG45664-4	#62 Kristy and the Worst Kid Ever	$3.50
❑ MG45665-2	#63 Claudia's Freind Friend	$3.50
❑ MG45666-0	#64 Dawn's Family Feud	$3.50
❑ MG45667-9	#65 Stacey's Big Crush	$3.50
❑ MG47004-3	#66 Maid Mary Anne	$3.50
❑ MG47005-1	#67 Dawn's Big Move	$3.50
❑ MG47006-X	#68 Jessi and the Bad Baby-Sitter	$3.50
❑ MG47007-8	#69 Get Well Soon, Mallory!	$3.50
❑ MG47008-6	#70 Stacey and the Cheerleaders	$3.50
❑ MG47009-4	#71 Claudia and the Perfect Boy	$3.50
❑ MG47010-8	#72 Dawn and the We Love Kids Club	$3.50
❑ MG45575-3	Logan's Story Special Edition Readers' Request	$3.25
❑ MG47118-X	Logan Bruno, Boy Baby-sitter Special Edition Readers' Request	$3.50
❑ MG44240-6	Baby-sitters on Board! Super Special #1	$3.95
❑ MG44239-2	Baby-sitters' Summer Vacation Super Special #2	$3.95
❑ MG43973-1	Baby-sitters' Winter Vacation Super Special #3	$3.95
❑ MG42493-9	Baby-sitters' Island Adventure Super Special #4	$3.95
❑ MG43575-2	California Girls! Super Special #5	$3.95
❑ MG43576-0	New York, New York! Super Special #6	$3.95
❑ MG44963-X	Snowbound Super Special #7	$3.95
❑ MG44962-X	Baby-sitters at Shadow Lake Super Special #8	$3.95
❑ MG45661-X	Starring the Baby-sitters Club Super Special #9	$3.95
❑ MG45674-1	Sea City, Here We Come! Super Special #10	$3.95

Available wherever you buy books...or use this order form.

Scholastic Inc., P.O. Box 7502, 2931 E. McCarty Street, Jefferson City, MO 65102

Please send me the books I have checked above. I am enclosing $_____
(please add $2.00 to cover shipping and handling). Send check or money order - no cash or C.O.D.s please.

Name _____ Birthdate_____

Address _____

City_____ State/Zip _____

Please allow four to six weeks for delivery. Offer good in the U.S. only. Sorry, mail orders are not available to residents of Canada. Prices subject to change.

THE **BIGGEST** BSC SWEE STAKES EVE !!

Scholastic and Ann M. Martin want to thank all of the Baby-sitters Club fans for a cool 100 million books in print! Celebrate by sending in your entry now!

ENTER AND YOU CAN WIN:

• *10 Grand Prizes:* Win one of ten $2,500 prizes! Your cash prize is good towards any artistic, academic, or sports pursuit. Take a dance workshop, go to soccer camp, get a violin tutor, learn a foreign language! You decide and Scholastic will pay the expense up to $2,500 value. Sponsored by Scholastic Inc., the Ann M. Martin Foundation, Kid Vision, Milton Bradley® and Kenner® Products.

• *100 First Prizes:* Win one of 100 fabulous runner-up gifts selected for you by Scholastic including a limited supply of BSC videos, autographed limited editions of Ann Martin's upcoming holiday book, T-shirts, board games and other fabulous merchandise!

Just fill in the coupon below or write the information on a 3" x 5" piece of paper and mail to: **THE BSC REMEMBERS SWEEPSTAKES**, Scholastic Inc., P.O. Box 7500, 2931 East McCarty Street, Jefferson City, MO 65102. Entries must be postmarked by 10/31/94.

Send to Scholastic Inc., P.O. Box 7500, 2931 East McCarty Street, Jefferson City, MO 65102.

THE BSC REMEMBERS SWEEPSTAKES

Name _____ Birthdate _____

Address _____ Phone# _____

City _____ State _____ Zip _____

Where did you buy this book? ❏ Bookstore   ❏ Other(Specify)

Name of Bookstore _____

BSCR19

ENTER SCHOLASTIC'S

THE BSC REMEMBERS
SWEEPSTAKES

Official Rules:

No purchase necessary. To enter use the official entry form or a 3" x 5" piece of paper and
hand print your full name, complete address, day telephone number and birthdate. Enter
as often as you wish, one entry to an envelope. Mechanically reproduced entries are void.
Mail to THE BSC REMEMBERS Sweepstakes at the address provided on the previous page,
postmarked by 10/31/94. Scholastic Inc. is not responsible for late, lost or postage due mail.
Sweepstakes open to residents of the U.S.A. 6-15 years old upon entering. Employees of
Scholastic Inc., Kid Vision, Milton Bradley Inc., Kenner Inc., Ann M. Martin Foundation,
their affiliates, subsidiaries, dealers, distributors, printers, mailers, and their immediate
families are ineligible. Prize winners will be randomly drawn from all eligible entries under
the supervision of Smiley Promotion Inc., an independent judging organization whose
decisions are final. Prizes: Ten Grand Prizes each $2,500 awarded toward any artistic,
academic or sports pursuit approved by Scholastic Inc. Winner may also choose $2,500
cash payment. An approved pursuit costing less than $2,500 must be verified by bona fide
invoice and presented to Scholastic Inc. prior to 7/31/95 to receive the cash difference. One
hundred First Prizes each a selection by Scholastic Inc. of BSC videos, Ann Martin books,
t-shirts and games. Estimated value each $10.00. Sweepstakes void where prohibited,
subject to all federal, state, provincial, local laws and regulations. Odds of winning depend
on the number of entries received. Prize winners are notified by mail. Grand Prize winners
and parent/legal guardian are mailed a Affidavit of Eligibility/ Liability/ Publicity/Release to
be executed and returned within 14 days of its date or an alternate winner may be drawn.
Only one prize allowed a person or household. Taxes on prize, expenses incurred outside
of prize provision and any injury, loss or damages incurred by acceptance and use of prizes
are the sole responsibility of the winners and their parent/legal guardian. Prizes cannot be
exchanged, transferred or cashed. Scholastic Inc. reserves the right to substitute prizes of
like value if any offered are unavailable and to use the names and likenesses of prize
winners without further compensation for advertising and promotional use. Prizes that are
unclaimed or undelivered to winner's address remain the property of Scholastic Inc. For a
Winners List, please send a stamped, addressed envelope to THE BSC REMEMBERS
Sweepstakes Winners, Smiley Promotion Inc., 271 Madison Avenue, #802, New York, N.Y.
10016 after 11/30/94. Residents of Washington state may omit return stamp.

Don't miss out on
The All New

**Wow! It's really them-
the new Baby-sitters Club dolls!**

Your favorite Baby-sitters Club characters have come to life in these
beautiful collector dolls. Each doll wears her own unique clothes and jewelry.
They look just like the girls you have imagined! The dolls also come with their own
individual stories in special edition booklets that you'll find nowhere else.

**Look for the new Baby-sitters Club collection...
coming soon to a store near you!**